Desert Moon

Book 1
The Wolves of Twin Moon Ranch

by Anna Lowe

Editing by Lisa A. Hollett

Covert art by Fiona Jayde Media
www.FionaJaydeMedia.com

Contents

Other books in this series

visit www.annalowebooks.com

Free Book

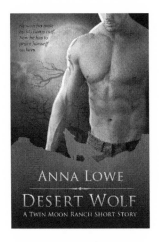

Desert Wolf

Get your free e-book now!

Sign up for my newsletter at *annalowebooks.com* to get your free copy of *Desert Wolf* (Book 1.1 in the series).

Lana Dixon may have won her destined mate's heart, but that was in Arizona. Now, she's bringing her desert wolf home to meet her family — the sworn enemies of his pack. How far will they push her mate to prove himself worthy? And is their relationship ready for the test?

Chapter One

Lana fidgeted next to her grandmother as the plane banked over the harsh landscape and slowly descended. *Arizona.* She almost muttered it aloud. She'd vowed never to return, and yet here she was.

The desert. All that open space, that sky. It had taken something out of her on her first visit, long ago, leaving her with a thirst she could never quench. So why go back?

The plane landed, and she moved stiffly to baggage claim, already wishing for a flight home. Catching herself grinding her teeth, she willed her jaws to relax. She would be calm and serene, damn it, even if she had to fake it. For one week, she could manage that much. She'd get her grandmother settled into her new home and then return to the East Coast. The desert had nothing for her.

She glued on a smile as an older woman hugged her grandmother, then turned to her with sparkling eyes and a secret smile.

"Lana, you look just like your mother!"

She gave a little internal sigh but didn't drop the forced smile. This must be Jean, her grandmother's old friend. She'd met Jean once before, but her memories of that time were hazy. All she remembered was the sense of loss her first visit had left her with. Which was crazy, because how could you lose something you never had?

"The eyes of her mother, the nose of her father," her grandmother winked, and Lana couldn't help but wonder what private joke they were sharing. But the older women breezed right over the subject and started chatting away about friends and family and times gone by. Lana tapped her foot, waiting for the baggage to roll past. The sooner she got this visit started, the sooner it would be over.

Twenty minutes later, she wheeled the luggage cart toward the exit, trailed by the older women. She sucked in a deep breath before stepping into the furnace outside the airport doors. The heat smothered her like a wool blanket, and the dry desert air seared her nostrils.

"One of Tyrone's boys is coming to get us," Jean said, looking up and down the road.

Lana looked too, gnawing her lip. It figured the kid would be late. While the two older women stood in the shade of a bus stop, catching up on twelve years of news, she paced. Out into the piercing sun, then back into the muted shade. Out and back, out and back again, each footfall a step into the past, then a determined about-face into the future. She tried to numb her senses, but they kept darting around, tasting the arid flavor of this place, listening to its emptiness. Everything felt so familiar, yet so strange, like visiting a childhood home after someone else had moved in.

That was the strange part. Arizona had never been her home and it never would be. She'd only visited once before. She went stiff at the memory, as if the old emotions might creep up and carry her away. Emotions like hope and love and unexpected passion, blazing bright. She'd been so young and impressionable back then. Only twenty, and that was the problem. Too young to know better than to fall in love with a vague scent in the hills. For a while, she'd even imagined the scent came with a man.

But it had been a siren song at best, and it had ruined her. There was no man, no promise, only a ceaseless whisper that stirred her during the day and haunted her at night. And now she was back again, right in the thick of it: the heat, the dust, the lying air.

"Oh, there he is," Jean called.

A faded Jeep Wagoneer pulled up to the curb and creaked to a stop. From what Jean had said, Lana had been expecting the driver to be a newly licensed teen—a kid delighted for any excuse to get out on four wheels. The type with narrow shoulders, a pocked complexion, and gangly limbs.

She was not expecting *this*.

Lana gaped as the "boy" emerged from the car with a smooth, easy step. Evidently the state of Arizona was now issuing driver's licenses to rugged, six-foot-two slabs of muscle and raw power. Authority bristled off him in waves, as if he were facing an entire platoon and not just a couple of guests. Dark. Sensual. More than a little dangerous. *This* was their ride?

"Hello, sweetie." Old Jean gave him a cheery peck on the cheek. The gesture made Lana's inner wolf hiss so fiercely that she wobbled and took a step back. Since when did a man affect her like that?

Since right now, apparently.

But why? She didn't want or need a man in her life, especially one who was so... so... alpha.

And yet every molecule in her body was screaming *Mine!*

∞∞∞∞

The last thing Ty needed was to play chauffeur to a couple of old women. He had a million things to do, not only in town but home on the ranch.

It always seemed like things came to a head when his father was away and he was on watch—a role he was taking on more and more often in a gradual changing of the guard. This time his father was in Utah for a week, give or take. Not that Ty minded the old man's absence or his chance to finally take charge. He was born to stand down the dangers threatening his pack: vampires, rogue wolves, and even humans. The latter were weak, but their overwhelming numbers and powerful fears made them an unpredictable risk.

Lately, though, it seemed as though the only problems he was being called upon to solve were petty quarrels that called for people skills, not power. *Not* his forte. Ty almost wished a real problem would arise to put things back in perspective. Then he could step into action and show them all.

3

He rejected the thought with a sharp shake of his head. His job wasn't to prove himself; it was to lead and ignore the rest. So what if it seemed that everyone was waiting—hoping, almost—for the first son of the alpha to show some weakness? It had been that way for as long as he could remember. The fact that he hadn't screwed up just upped the ante: now they expected perfection. Was he a wolf, or a magician?

Ty forced himself to take a deep breath. He was his father's son. He would do a good job—even better than his father, if that were possible.

So what the hell was he doing as taxi driver to a couple of old women?

That question, he could answer. Aunt Jean—his great-aunt, actually—had practically raised him. She was the only person other than his father who could give him an order, even though hers came covered in cream and honey and with a tickle of the cheek as if he were still a cub. So ninety minutes ago, he had dropped her off at the airport to await her friend before going off on his own errands, gnashing his teeth the whole time. Now he pulled up outside the arrivals area, tapping his fingers on the wheel. Where were they?

Then he spotted Jean with a heap of luggage, chatting in the shade of a bus stop with another gray-haired woman. He stifled a yawn, picturing the cobwebs of their conversation. Too bad they weren't with that leggy brunette who was pacing nearby. The one with the chiseled calves and no-nonsense stride. Now *that* would be his kind of chauffeuring. Or more like his womanizing brother's kind of chauffeuring, because he wouldn't allow himself to be affected by any woman again.

Not even this one.

Except that he sniffed as he drove past, trying to tease her scent out of the complex symphony of city smells.

What if. . . what if. . . his wolf tried.

Part of him quivered in hope; the other part snorted in disgust. *Give it up.* It wasn't as if the woman he'd lost his heart to so long ago would simply walk back into his life.

He killed the engine and unfolded himself from the cab.

"Ty, sweetie, this is my dear friend Ruth," Aunt Jean said.

"I remember you as a little cub!" Ruth exclaimed. "My, how you've grown."

He squeezed his lips and endured.

"And this is my granddaughter, Lana." She gestured to somebody standing behind him.

He turned and found himself stuck midway between inhaling and exhaling. It was her—the brunette, wearing light capris and a V-neck T-shirt that offered the barest hint of an athletic figure. She looked to be about thirty, a little younger than him. There was neither a brush of make-up on her face, nor a speck of jewelry in sight. She didn't need any. She was perfect just the way she was.

Luckily, she was a little slow to react, because his joints seized up along with his breath. When her hand finally reached out to grip his in greeting, all his synapses fired simultaneously.

"Hi," she said in that clipped East Coast way. Her eyes locked onto his, wide and blue as the desert sky after a welcome rain. He felt dragged in, dropping like a skydiver. The hand she offered was warm and fit his so perfectly, he couldn't let go.

A voice vaguely registered behind the roaring in his ears. "Get the luggage, sweetie," Jean called, one foot already in the car.

Luggage? Right. He snatched a bag off the cart and loaded it into the Jeep. Then he turned for the next one, taking it from Lana's hand. It was a light, sporty duffel, not a girly thing; either she packed ultra-light or she wasn't planning on staying long. The layers of muscle surrounding his ribs tightened at the thought.

"I can get it." Her protest came too late. When he spun back to face her, her eyes were swirling like the sky before a summer storm, angry as all hell.

He got caught up in that tempest for a moment before she let out a muffled growl that snapped him back to the moment. Crap. She must be one of those stubborn, independent types capable of opening her own doors and giving herself a hernia carrying heavy things just to prove she could. One of those stubborn women who. . . who had the most enticing scent. Fresh. Promising, like a west wind. Familiar, almost.

He was still savoring her scent when Lana pushed past him and heaved another bag into the car. Great. He'd managed to antagonize her already.

He pulled his lower lip in tight and clenched his jaw. He was good at that—pissing people off. Keeping them safely at arm's length. Too bad she was one of the few he might be interested in keeping close. Very close.

He slammed the door a little too hard, cursing the long drive home.

∞∞∞∞

Within minutes, he was shifting around and wishing for his own truck. But since his open-bed pickup was hardly the vehicle for chauffeuring old ladies, here he was, stuck in one of the ranch cars.

It wasn't just the vehicle, though. Lana was driving him crazy, sitting right behind him while the older women crooned on about old times. With the wind whipping through the open window, he couldn't quite capture her scent. Her posture was stiff, her expression carefully schooled. Everything about this woman spoke of discipline and control. She was pretty, too, in her wildcat kind of way that made him hungry to know more.

He wanted to say something, just to hear more of her voice. But words had never been his thing, so he tightened his hands around the steering wheel and resigned himself to a long drive.

As they left the heat of the city for the cooler, higher altitudes of the north, Lana sat as taut as an over-tensioned spring. She appeared to be caught between wanting to inhale all of northern Arizona and forcing herself to hold back. He knew that feeling intimately. Keeping passion a slave to self-discipline, never letting too much of yourself show. He knew why he did it, but why did she?

"Maybe when we get to the ranch, you can show Lana around," Aunt Jean chirped.

I can definitely show her around, his wolf murmured. *And I bet she can show me a thing or two, too.*

He leashed his inner animal and dragged it kicking and screaming into one of those stupid pet crates provided by his imagination. He could practically hear the scrape of claws across a slippery linoleum floor. Then his eyes strayed to Lana's in the rear view mirror, and promptly vaulted away. He would definitely not be showing this woman anything.

"Got work," he grunted—and immediately regretted it. Resisting his pack's matchmaking efforts was second nature to him by now. Even his father had pulled a little stunt a few years back, trying to stick him with an arranged mate. He bit back a growl just thinking about it. What little private life he had was none of their business. He'd found and lost his destined mate. There could be no other. Case closed.

"Oh, Lana," her grandmother chirped from the front seat. "Look at the pretty cactus."

Lana leaned forward to see, and her hair swayed tantalizingly close to his shoulder. He swallowed, hard.

"And oh—what a magnificent falcon!" Ruth went on.

Just as Lana ducked to get a view out the windshield, the truck hit a bump, and her hand gripped the seat at his shoulder, making his blood surge through his veins.

The drive stretched on in the same way, every mile a tease and torture. Lana barely uttered a sound, and he was tempted to start up his own commentary, just to see how she reacted.

Lana, he'd say, *see those hills? Behind them is where we're headed.* She'd lean so close he might even feel her sweet breath in his ear. *That's the ranch. A little rough around the edges, but the most beautiful place on earth.*

He wanted to hear her coo in wonder and squint for a better view. Wanted her to know what the place meant to him.

Or maybe he'd say, *Lana, you should see it in spring, when the desert's in bloom* Then maybe she'd turn her head from left to right, glowing in wonder in spite of herself, just like he used to do when he was little.

He wanted to throw an arm across the back of his seat, twist around to glance at her—right at her—and say, *Lana, you remind me of someone, only I don't know who.*

He got as far as releasing his death grip on the wheel with one hand and opening his mouth. Lana leaned forward on cue, her eyes following his lips in the rear-view mirror, her head tilting to catch his unspoken words. An instant later, she caught her blunder and threw herself back into her seat, crossing her arms over her chest in self-defense.

He sighed. Like he'd even manage a full sentence around her. Not with his pulse spiking just watching her. Not with her studying everything in the desert but him.

Ruth gestured out the windows at the last of Phoenix's outlying suburbs. "I can't believe how the city has grown," she said. "Remember it, Lana?"

He was all ears. What was there for her to remember?

Lana murmured vaguely. Had she been there before? His mind went into a digging spree, throwing dirt everywhere without managing to find any trace of her. Then Ruth shifted to another topic, and his chance to ask was gone. Probably the old woman was simply mixed up. He would have remembered if Lana had been in Arizona before. He would definitely remember.

Every animal instinct in him was stirring, wanting to touch and taste her. To pull her out of this truck and over to some private place where he could study her up close and personal. And not just her body. The rest, too. What was going on in her mind? Her heart? Her soul?

It was a feeling he hadn't had in... how long? Of course there were other women who'd managed to get him going, but that feeling was pretty much limited to his cock. This woman called to something much deeper. He didn't so much want to lay her as to... what? What did he want?

To get to know her. To figure her out. That's what he wanted.

Okay, okay, and to lay her, too.

Who was she? How dare she have such an effect on him? Because no one did this to him. No one! Not since the phantom—and she didn't exist.

Chapter Two

Twenty miles into the drive, Lana was still trying to reconcile the boy Jean had led her to expect, versus the man in the car. The very real, very grown-up man.

Gangly, my ass.

She had watched him lean over a bag and hoist it up as if it were feather light. Nice, tight buns filled his jeans, and his biceps bulged under the cuffs of his white T-shirt. No tan lines around the edges, either, making it all too easy to picture him shirtless, letting the sun bronze his skin. But then he'd taken the next bag right out of her hand, and her vision had gone red.

Alphas. They had the people skills of Neanderthals. As the daughter of one and sister to three others, she should know. Alpha males were all the same.

Except this one was the finest thing she had ever seen. Deeply tanned with brown-black hair, the man was downright delicious, like dark chocolate ice cream with molten fudge on top. What she wouldn't give to dip right in. His face wasn't so much handsome as it was enticing, but his lips were pursed, his brow creased. His thick shoulders were squared as if he was about to challenge an adversary. Was he always so tense?

And did he always smell so good? He'd showered with something very, very masculine. It smelled like the desert: edgy and brutally honest. Or maybe that wasn't soap, but just him.

A scowl crossed her face, and she couldn't help but wonder if the local girls had some kind of lottery system for who got to share his bed. Or did he stick with just one? She doubted it. You could tell a mated wolf from a mile away; peace and

9

satisfaction sloughed off him in waves. Ty was too restless, too brooding for that.

She sniffed again. A man like him ought to carry the scent of half a dozen recent conquests, like a magic potion of virility that only served to attract more. His partners would probably make damn sure they rubbed him close and hard to leave their mark for the world to witness. She pictured a wall of graffiti, sprayed all over. *Cyndi was here*, it would say, and that would overlap with *Ty + Lucy*, written inside a heart, or maybe *Kerri loves Ty*, with part of the *Kerri* gouged out by some jealous soul.

She sniffed again and was surprised to find no trace of a recent female scent intertwined with his. If anything, the man smelled like duty and responsibility. An alpha, through and through.

She gave her head an inner shake and tried to pry her senses away. But this man sucked her in like no man ever before. She suddenly understood what birds must feel when they flew south. She was being pulled, like Mother Nature was pointing and uttering urgently: *Him! Him!*

But whenever she worked up the nerve to throw a covert glance his way, he seemed to retreat further into his invisible armor, curling tighter and tighter until his emotions were as safely guarded as an armadillo in a ball.

She forced herself back in her seat, as far as she could. The guy was way too intense. Too... too everything. Wasn't her mother always warning her about alphas?

The Wagoneer left city congestion behind, heading north into open desert. She had resolved to resist the call of the landscape, but since it now seemed the lesser of two temptations, she peered out the window. Prickly pears blurred past, and a scattering of saguaro cacti gave way to scrappy bush as the highway climbed. Every plant clung to its patch of scorched earth, struggling to survive. Yet there was something here that whispered to her, as it had on her first visit. The realization both thrilled and frightened her.

As did Ty. Her senses couldn't resist throwing themselves at him—not just peeking but measuring, studying, imprinting the details in her mind like the last days of summer.

A good thing it was cooler up here at higher altitude than in the city. The Jeep struggled with a steep incline that she vaguely remembered from her first trip. Out of the corner of her eye, she saw an incongruous flash of red in the arid landscape. A sports car was pulling alongside the Jeep. It was so close and so loud the bass notes of its stereo thumped in her bones. Lana checked Ty's expression in the rear view mirror, but his mouth remained straight, unrevealing.

With a boastful rev, the sports car sped ahead. Any one of Lana's brothers would have hurled a comment after it, but Ty's only reaction, if it was one, was a quick scratch of his ear. Then his hand was back on the wheel, knuckles clenched white.

An hour passed; it seemed an eternity. She wondered how was she going to last a week around him.

"Not far now," Jean said.

Lana closed her eyes. *Already way too close.*

Ty turned off the highway and onto an unmarked dirt road. Like all wolf packs, Ty's kept their presence discrete. No sense in calling human attention to themselves.

It was in the turn that she noticed the flaring of Ty's nostrils. She could feel it, too. Something was wrong. Ty's jawline tightened ever so slightly, though he didn't show a nervous twitch or rub an imaginary beard. The tension was there though: she could see it in the pinch of his shoulders, the tight grip of his fingers on the wheel—and there—another scratch at his right ear.

Incredible. The man was so bottled up that his only outlet was scratching an ear. His eyes slid left, eying a spot high in the hills, and though she followed his gaze, she saw nothing. What was up there that he wanted to escape to?

She glanced around the vehicle. Did no one else pick up on it? The older women seemed oblivious. Was it always like that? Ty hid his feelings so well, it was almost as if they didn't exist. But she saw. He was a man, not a machine, caged in by the heavy weight of responsibility.

The Jeep crossed over a low bridge that spanned the cracked remnants of a creek then slowed to pass under a timber gateway. The ranch brand hung overhead: two circles, side by side, overlapping by one-third. By the looks of things, Twin Moon Ranch hadn't changed a bit. The same cottonwoods shaded two rows of buildings on either side of a central square. Take away the trucks and it would pass for a movie set, but she knew this was the real thing. The Wild West come true.

The five men who were huddled on the porch of the first building on the right turned toward the car in anticipation. Judging by the barbed look on their faces, there was serious pack business to discuss.

Ty did it again, one quick scratch, and she was seized with the urge to take that ear and lick it smooth, to blow the worries away. Alphas ruled at the top, but they stood alone. While victories were shared, the specter of defeat loomed over the individual. Ty had the same brooding aura.

Most alphas found release through the support of siblings or a mate, not to mention the occasional brawl. But this man was the type to build a bigger and bigger dam, trying to hold everything inside. She wanted to reach over the seat, knead his shoulders, and whisper something reassuring in his ear. But how could she? He was a stranger, after all, and she was just passing through.

Ty rolled the pickup to a near stop as one of the men approached, and they seemed to communicate volumes in the brief nods they exchanged.

Jean called out a chipper greeting. "Hello, Cody, sweetheart!"

The blond man broke into a winning smile and waved. He looked out of place among the others. A bit too young and jolly for this setting. He belonged out in the surf on a Californian beach, not on a ranch. She would bet that women lined up for him in droves, but she only had eyes for Ty. This feeling of being fully awake and alive hadn't coursed through her blood in years. No surfer dude could do that.

Ty concluded his private exchange and continued to a T, then turned left, cruising past several houses and barns. Everything about the place was as she remembered it: a tidy community of lawns and winding irrigation ditches that faded into paddocks and open land. In a deeply troubled world, Twin Moon Ranch seemed like a shady little pocket of paradise. How much of that was a mirage?

Ty unloaded the two older women and luggage at Jean's duplex, then nodded her back to the car. "You're in the guest house," he said. His tone supplied the rest: *Let's go. I have things to do.*

"I can find it," she insisted.

"I'll take you." *Get in the car.*

She crossed her arms and she stood scowling. One of the first things he'd said to her, and it was an order. But then again, what did she expect?

It was only the memory of the group of men waiting for Ty that made her slide into the front seat and clamp down on her tongue. In two minutes, Ty had the truck parked in the central square. The men looked over expectantly, but Ty ignored them. He grabbed her bag before she could protest and pointed her toward a narrow path between two buildings. Ahead of them, thick shrubbery shaded a tiny adobe dwelling with a slanted roof and a stone chimney that clung to one wall like a determined vine. She took two quick steps over the creaky wooden porch, then stopped in front of the door, breathing in the hot spice of the chili peppers strung there.

The floorboards squeaked behind her as Ty came near. She could feel the heat of him. So close.

She turned instinctively and took him in. His hair looked just long enough for her fingers to skim through for a short ride. She imagined how close she'd have to be to do that. Close enough to feel the scrape of his stubble. To taste those lips. Close enough to nuzzle him until the edge had gone out of his taut body. Close enough to let their bodies brush, mesh, intertwine—

"It's open." His voice was gruff.

She forced herself to pull it together. God, her wolf was out of control today.

The screen door gave a rusty squeal as she stepped inside and forced her attention there. The heavy beams overhead smelled of wood oil and time. The walls were white, the ceiling high. A painting of a rose hung over the bed, whispering of reckless possibility.

Ty set down her bag, and when their eyes locked as he straightened, the whisper became a roar. She got lost in his deep, dark gaze. The chiseled line of his jaw pulsed with unspoken words. She was frozen, yet burning up at the same time. The moment stretched to infinity as the air throbbed and hummed in her ears. Was her heart barely pulsing or was it thumping like a rabbit's? There was some secret communication between them—a question asked and answered—though her mind couldn't register what that might be. They were mere puppets, bystanders to some greater reckoning.

Then Ty's eyes dropped to the floor and the earth stilled. Her mind took a moment to catch up, and by the time it did, the screen door had slammed. He was gone.

She slumped to the bed, her heart hammering, her ears vaguely registering the bang of the screen door. A bead of sweat dropped in slow motion from her brow. She'd survived a brush with a tornado and was still reeling, wondering how close it had come to whirling her away.

For the first time in a long while, she wanted to believe in the wolfpack myths. That there was love at first sight. That she would find her destined mate and the air would shimmer and rush. That her heat would reach out and intertwine with his and they'd slam together in a living storm of passion and never ever part.

But this man might as well have barbed wire coiled around his torso and a danger sign around his neck. *Warning! Death by hundreds of thousands of volts.* She wondered if Ty had rigged the defense system himself or some outside force had done it for him.

Her breathing slowly settled as her mind jerked on the reins. Maybe Ty had that effect on everyone. A powerful alpha could do that—melt everyone and everything in his path. Either you'd self-incinerate or he'd kill you the slow way: death by broken heart.

Best to avoid him. The man was bossy, busy, and seriously wounded. A man like that needed a lot of fixing—and hell, she was no mechanic.

And anyway, a myth was a myth. There was no such thing as a destined mate, not these days anyway. Shifters who found mates did it the clumsy human way: trial by error. Guessing, trying, compromising. And even that took time, patience, and hope—three things she just didn't possess. This crazy stirring inside her soul was just her wolf hearing the call of the desert, and that could be explained by the half of her DNA that came from her Arizona-born mother.

Either way, it didn't matter. She could damn well control her urges. A woman had to have some pride, after all. She shook the image of Ty out of her brain and promised herself she'd concentrate on what she came for, then get the hell out of Arizona.

And never come back.

Chapter Three

Ty strode away from the adobe cabin, sucking in the breath he'd forgotten to draw back there. He'd only barely broken away and his wolf was still scratching madly to escape.

Take her, it growled. *You know you want her.*

He did. Badly. And she felt the same way. One touch and she'd be his. He could feel it.

Take her now!

He wanted—needed—her like a drunk needed a drink. She could set him free. Maybe set them both free.

Take her!

Jesus, his hands were shaking. Not from proximity to danger or a foe, but from her. Only one other woman had ever had this effect on him.

The phantom.

It happened years ago, after he'd been away from the ranch on business. The minute he got back, it hit like a heat wave in the height of summer. A scent. A female scent carried on the wind touched him—no, kneed him right in the gut—then vanished. Overcome by the need to claim, he'd roamed all over the desert. He spent weeks searching, every keen wolf sense tuned in to tracking the source. But she was gone—or she never existed, except as a hint on the wind that teased him to ruin. He'd never love, never want anyone again.

The itch, the longing never really faded. It came and went in unpredictable waves, like seasons gone wrong.

Now Lana's scent was calling to him in exactly the same way. He had been on the verge of reaching for her in the guest house and only barely managed to stop himself. Men like him—like his father—were dangerous. Their intensity drained

17

anyone they let too near. If he took Lana as his mate, he would suck the life out of her, bit by bit. Like his father had done to all his women. One after another, they had all wilted under that intensity. Ty's mother was stronger than the others, and she'd left before it was too late, abandoning her kids for Aunt Jean to raise. Whenever he dropped one bedmate, his father would move on to a new woman, and then another one. Shifters could live two to three hundred years but pureblooded weres had a notoriously hard time conceiving. Which was good, in a way; Ty figured he might have had dozens of half-siblings if that weren't the case. His father never found the one woman who could balance him and make him whole.

They said the more powerful the alpha, the harder it was to find a mate, and he believed it. If Lana wasn't his destined mate—and how could she be, if she wasn't the phantom?—she'd eventually wilt away, too. Oh, she would put up a good fight. She had met his eyes and actually held his gaze. Very few people could do that. His own siblings had trouble looking at him when he was fired up. Everyone else stared at some point on his forehead or shoulder, or simply looked away.

Power was a curse. He'd always stand alone.

But what if? A tantalizing array of images flitted through his mind. What if Lana could withstand that force? She would give him a life outside of work and duty. A life worth living.

If only her scent matched that of the phantom! Then he could throw all doubt aside and take her as he'd nearly done in the guest house. He'd pull her close, find that spot on her neck. His teeth would slip right in and barely draw a drop of blood as he held on, letting their life essences intertwine. That would claim her and mark her as his forever. She wanted it, too; he could feel it.

But the scents didn't match. Not exactly. And if the stories were true, a wolf recognized his destined mate on first sight. So if he was unsure, it meant he could be wrong about both Lana and the phantom. Maybe there was no destined mate for him. Aunt Jean had never found one; neither had his father, and any number of other wolves. Some eventually settled for mating with whoever they decided was good enough and did their best to make it work. An ordinary mate; an ordinary relationship. No fireworks, no bonding of souls, no perfect match. Nothing like destined mates.

He kicked a rut into the dirt road. The hand he ran through his hair came out damp with sweat, and he huffed at his own helplessness. The big bad alpha, floored by a woman he hadn't even touched.

He fought off the memory of having her close and stepped to the Jeep, reaching down to close the tailgate. He had to get to that meeting. But instead of lifting, his arms leaned down to prop up his stiff frame. Hell, he was the one who was drained. Even breathing took a conscious effort.

Tick, said one second. *Everyone is waiting.*

Tock, said the next. *She could change your life.*

Tick.

Tock.

Someone across the way coughed quietly. Ty's ear twitched, and the moment was over. Duty called. He'd never failed his pack, and never would. No matter what it cost him.

He slammed the tailgate closed and strode across the square.

∞∞∞

Cody met him with a wicked look only he would pull at a time like this. He shot a rueful laugh into Ty's mind, as all packmates could, along with a clear message.

Who was that cute chick? Maybe I'll show her around after—

Ty thumped Cody on the chest by way of greeting, hard enough to knock his brother back a step.

Cody's eyes went wide. *She's all yours, bro.*

Ty's wolf snarled back before he could leash it. *Yes. Yes she is.*

Christ, that set it all off again. His blood volume seemed to double at the very thought of Lana. It was the worst possible time to get distracted. He had pressing business—very

19

pressing, from the looks of those waiting outside the council house.

Ty nodded to their visitor: Atsa, alpha of the neighboring coyote pack. In human form, Atsa had the wiry stature and distinctive features of his Navajo people, plus the keen eyes of his namesake, the eagle. In coyote form, the man was quick and wily despite his years. Ty held the door for the coyote elder, then followed him inside the council house, leading the way for the other coyote and wolf shifters gathered there.

The wooden building stood a few feet above ground level to let cool air circulate underneath. A low, sloping roof kept out both the sun and prying eyes. Benches lined both sides of the interior, while the middle was left open. He glanced around the uncluttered space, wishing everything in his life could be that way.

Tina, his sister, was already there, wearing her trademark no-nonsense look. She sat in her usual spot to the right of their father's heavy oak chair. Ty stood stiffly in front of the empty chair while Cody filed into the room, followed by several of their senior packmates.

Ty nodded to Atsa to start, and their visitor came right to the point.

"You've heard the reports."

Oh, he'd heard the reports, all right. He reminded himself not to growl in frustration. Atsa's coyote pack were good neighbors. Although the wolves were relative newcomers to this region, having only staked their claim two centuries ago, the packs had learned to coexist. Keeping humans ignorant of their true nature was one common interest; controlling any incursions by rogue shifters was another.

"Yes, I've heard."

Over the past two weeks, reports of rogue activity had been trickling in: a few dead sheep here, a human murdered there. Ty knew as well as Atsa did that most shifters were peaceable and law-abiding souls who lived by a strict code of honor—one that many humans could stand to emulate. Rogues, however, recognized no laws, pack or human.

"You remember Yas?" The name thudded off Atsa's tongue.

Ty nodded. The white coyote—hence his name: Yas, or Snow. Yas had always stirred up trouble. *White men invaded our land,* he'd rant. *They must be driven away. Wolves are arrogant bastards who don't deserve to share our ancestral lands.* Yas had even struck out at his own kind within the coyote pack. Eventually, things went too far and a fellow shifter was killed. As great-grandson of the coyote alpha, Yas received the relatively light sentence of banishment. Death would have been the wiser choice.

"I remember," Ty grumbled, grinding his teeth over every word.

Atsa sighed, and every line on his ancient face deepened. "It is he who stirs up trouble. Scouts believe they have caught his scent to the west. Yas, and others who are... unclean."

"Rogues," Ty corrected, and all eyes jumped to him. Why dance around the point? Rogues were rogues, and the danger was real. He returned each look with his own burning stare until each and every man dropped his eyes in submission. Then he glanced back at Atsa, tempering his stare for the old man. An elder was an elder, to be respected and revered even if the old man didn't keep his pack as tightly disciplined as Ty would have liked. "Where are they now?"

Tina folded and re-folded her hands at the periphery of his vision, signaling for him to stay cool. His sister, the diplomat.

Atsa's expression conveyed the weariness of a man betrayed. "They cover their tracks well and move quickly..."

If it had been a man of lesser standing beating around the bush, Ty would have snapped. He settled for a pointed stare, feeling his packmates' scrutiny. It had become so familiar, this sense of a collectively held breath, of an audience leaning forward, hoping to see the trapeze artist fall. Would Ty prove himself a worthy successor to his father?

"And?" His prompt came out as a bark, aimed more at his packmates than Atsa.

"And..." The senior coyote shook his head. "I fear he plans to come home. And not alone."

"Home." Ty made it a statement, not a question. Yas hadn't been seen or heard from in years. And coming back... That shouldn't be possible. Yas could never come home. If he tried, there'd be more trouble, more bloodshed. Then again, that might be just what Yas was after.

If the threat had come from any other rogue, he wouldn't be as concerned. But Yas was ambitious. Clever. Pure evil and only half sane. Oh yes, Ty remembered him well.

He let Atsa's silence say the rest. The coyotes had no idea where or when the rogues might strike. Coyotes were notoriously hard to track—harder even than the cleverest wolf.

He turned to Cody. "When are Zack and Rae due back?" Surely the pack's best tracker and his skilled huntress of a mate could root out the rogues—if they got back from Wyoming in time.

Cody gave an apologetic shake of his head, side to side. "Not for another week. And we haven't been able to get in touch."

He bit back a curse. Just when the pack needed their expertise most... and he could use Zack's steady presence just about now. Hell, he could use a trip of his own sometime, and a mate to go with him.

He jutted his chin left, then right. No use wishing for what he couldn't have. An alpha led, and led alone.

"Send out the scouts," he told Cody, cold and curt, just the way his father delivered orders. "Double the patrols."

When Cody nodded and strode out of the council house, Ty made a mental note to check his brother's thoroughness the minute the meeting ended, just in case. Because with Cody, you never knew.

The door to the council house opened, emitting a thick shaft of sunshine that spotlit the knotted pinewood floor. Ty let his eyes drift for a moment, then cleared his throat. "We'll keep each other informed," he grunted then dismissed Atsa with a nod and a downward flick of his eyes. Ty's father wouldn't have bothered with the gesture. As alpha of Twin Moon pack and host of this meeting, he didn't have to offer old Atsa that extra sign of respect. But the coyote was as old as the hills, and Aunt Jean had taught him to respect that generation. In part, he had to admit to some fascination, too. Atsa's inner calm intrigued him, the antithesis of his father's blustery style.

He sensed Atsa studying him, and wondered whether the old coyote approved of him as Twin Moon's new alpha. Of course, his father was still nominally in charge, but everyone knew the handover of power had already begun.

Atsa gave a cryptic nod and made for the open door then for his truck outside. In forty minutes, the old coot would be back on his home turf, west of the ranch. South of their territories was Seymour Ranch, whose human owners were ignorant of their neighbors' special abilities. The northern edge of wolf country melted into the rugged hills, unclaimed and largely unwanted land, and the highway delineated the eastern edge of their realm. Trouble in the form of rogues could come from any direction, and the pack would have to protect everyone. Humans, too. If the rogues started taking outside victims, there'd be investigations, unwanted attention.

He ignored Tina's hint of a cough. The others assembled in the council house could wait for his dismissal until he was good and ready to give it.

As the coyotes drove off, he shook his head. Had he really been wishing for a challenge? Now he had it—trouble on two fronts. His eyes slid in the direction of the guest house.

There couldn't have been a worse time.

Chapter Four

The dining hall was filled with aroma and noise: the honey-tinged fragrance of roast ham, the sugary smell of sweet potato, the babble of voices. But all Ty heard—or tasted—were hushed tones and whispered warnings. Communal dinner night was a twice-weekly event at the ranch, and for him, it was a chance to discretely touch base with his most trusted men. Ty wanted them to be ready for the worst while keeping news of the rogues quiet. There was no need to alarm the others.

Yet.

Around him, voices chattered, plates clattered. Most of the hundred-plus shifters living locally were in the dining hall, plus a few from more isolated parts of the ranch. Like Kyle, the cop turned shifter who was approaching the head table now. Kyle was the newest member of the pack, and he hadn't settled in yet—if he ever would. You could tell from the twitch of his eyes, his constantly clenched jaw. If it hadn't been for Tina's soft spot for outcasts, a loose cannon like Kyle would never have been admitted to the pack. But Tina had been right to back him. Kyle hadn't caused any trouble, except maybe for stirring up jealous rivalries among the women. He'd proven valuable time and time again, providing inside information from state law enforcement agencies.

"You've got nothing?" Ty demanded, keeping his voice pitched low. Not that anyone dared sit close enough to him to overhear... at least not without an invitation. Only Tina, who tilted the vegetable bowl at him in another hint. Although she was younger than him, she'd started mothering him a long time ago.

Kyle shook his head bitterly. The man hated failure nearly

as much as Ty did. "Nothing to pin down the rogu—" he broke off the word sharply, perhaps considering how close he himself had come to turning rogue. He looked around, then leaned closer. "Not yet."

"Not yet," Ty muttered, then dismissed Kyle with a curt wave.

A little too curt, maybe. He caught the sag in Kyle's shoulders, the tightening of his jaw. A reaction he'd seen a thousand times when packmates turned away with his father. His shoulders stiffened. Did he really want to be the same way?

"Just keep on it," he added, a little softer than before. His version of soft was still on the pebbly side, but hell, at least he was trying.

Kyle's cheek quirked—the closest either one of them ever got to a smile—and he turned and left.

Ty glanced down to find mere scraps on his plate and tried to recall what he'd just shoveled down for dinner. He could barely remember going through the motions of eating. Well, rogue or no rogue, he wouldn't let dessert get by him that easily. Not with key lime pie on the menu. He shoved back from the table and stalked across the room, barely acknowledging the packmates scurrying out of his way.

Cody was already at the dessert table, helping himself to a double serving as he joked to the person next to him. "Aren't you worried about getting fat?"

Ty stiffened when he saw who it was: Lana, waiting her turn. She crinkled her nose at the comment. "You're the one with two pieces."

Sassy thing. She'd probably burn through a thousand calories just fidgeting at the table.

Sensing his presence, Cody froze, then grabbed the nearest woman and made a quick exit. "Beth, honey! Going to the movie tonight?"

Lana watched them go with an amused expression that faltered the moment she spotted Ty.

"Hi," she mumbled, her eyes meeting his. The blue hues of her irises were so varied and vivid, he could swear they were swirling and changing as he looked on.

"Hi," he said. Well, he tried to. His lips moved but the sound didn't quite make it out. He struggled to remember where he was and why.

Right, dessert. He reached for a piece of pie exactly when Lana did. Their hands froze halfway to the platter, both wavering over the key lime pie. The last slice.

"Cody!" He cursed under his breath.

Lana pulled back. "You take it."

"No, you."

Her eyes narrowed at him. Crap. He hadn't meant for it to come out as an order, but she was already gritting her teeth.

"No, you," she ground out.

"I'm good." He tried taking the edge off his voice, but he was badly out of practice.

Lana studied him so closely he would swear she could see into his childhood memories. Her nostrils flared, and he saw her catch a breath and hold it. Then she slowly exhaled and turned to the platter, scooping the last piece onto the last plate. She forked it roughly in half and held it between them with icy determination.

"We'll share," she growled.

The alpha in him both bristled and admired her pluck. The wolf licked his lips—and not for the pie.

Her eyes flickered, focusing on something in his. He noticed an outer edge of green in her eyes that he'd missed before, like the foam that slid off the crests of waves.

"Trouble today?" she asked, keeping her voice down.

Trouble? So she'd noticed the meeting. "No trouble," he insisted.

She snorted. "I do that, too."

"Do what?"

"Pretend."

Ty blinked. "I don't pretend."

"Then what's the trouble?" She took a bite of pie and licked a smudge of cream off her lips.

A breath caught in his throat, and a word slipped past his lips before he could catch it. "Rogues."

Her face hardened as some dark memory rocketed through her eyes. "Confirmed report?"

"Not yet, but..."

She nodded, letting him trail off. In an absent movement, her right arm rubbed briefly over her left, where a wicked scar trailed out of her sleeve.

"Trouble?" he murmured, eyes on the scar. For a shifter to scar, it must have been bad.

She yanked the sleeve down. "No trouble."

I do that, too, he wanted to say. *Pretend.* His gut warmed with something strangely close to pride. This East Coast wolf wasn't just sassy; she was tough.

Lana shrugged and brought her fork up to her mouth. "You should see the rogue who gave me that scar. Except he's dead, along with his pals." She took a vengeful bite.

He wondered just how many rogues there'd been against how many on Lana's side. He was about to ask when a voice shoved between them, wielding a sledgehammer.

"Ty! Ty!" He felt a soft arm slink around his and fought the instinct to flinch. "Ty, I've missed you," Audrey murmured, her tongue all but making contact with his ear. He eased out an elbow, trying to edge away from her fleshy breasts. The bleached blonde turned to give Lana a predatory smile. "Aren't you going to introduce us, Ty?"

He cast a desperate eye around the dining hall. Where was Cody when he needed him? "Audrey, meet Lana," he murmured, searching for a way out.

"Hmpf," Audrey said by way of greeting. "You'll get fat eating all that pie."

He could tell a retort was trying to itch its way out of Lana, but she swallowed it along with another bite of the pie. He needed to brush Audrey off, pronto. What if Lana thought he actually went for Audrey's type? He shot a mental command across the room. *Cody, get your ass back here now!*

"Staying long?" Audrey asked of Lana. His ears leaped to attention.

"Just a few days."

Why the rush?

"Will we see you later?" Audrey asked. "It's movie night, you know." She nestled closer and gave him a bedroom look, like she couldn't wait for the lights to go down. "You're coming, aren't you, Ty?"

He shook his head. "Work." Thank God.

"We have our own little theater, you know," Audrey boasted to Lana. "The boys converted the old barn."

"Nice." Lana nodded. "But I prefer open space."

His wolf perked up his ears, liking what he heard.

"So you won't be coming?" Audrey didn't sound disappointed. "Too bad. You could stuff your face with all the popcorn you like."

Lana sidestepped the jab. "I need to run."

God, I could use a run, too.

"Are you sure that's safe?" Audrey asked, looking hopeful that it wasn't.

"Just keep to the property," he said.

Lana nodded, venturing the slightest smile. Ty itched to reach out and coax the rest out of her, but his fists stayed clenched by his sides.

"Audrey!" Cody appeared, flashing a Broadway grin. The cavalry had finally arrived. "How's my girl?" he said, stooping to give Audrey a peck on the cheek.

She gave him a halfhearted kiss. "One of your girls, you mean."

"Life is short, sweetheart." With a wink that could have been aimed at Ty, Lana, or Hollywood, Cody danced Audrey away, murmuring about back row seats in the theater.

They slipped out of the periphery of his vision and immediately ceased to exist, at least as far as he was concerned. The room began to hum and throb, and his vision narrowed to a tunnel that pushed out everything but Lana. Her eyes pulled him in and made his heart thump low and hard. Or was that her heart? They were only inches apart now. The air shimmered around them like noontime heat over the desert. When she leaned closer, his wolf whined. What he wouldn't give to circle her now, rub along her side—

"Ty!" A cacophony of voices and clinking tableware suddenly filled his ears. Kyle was approaching him, and the room was pulling back into focus. "Ty, about the patrols..."

In his haze, he felt Lana press the dessert plate into his hands and slip away. He reached for her too late, his hand clutching air, then balling into a fist. His body ached with every step she took, and he willed her eyes to touch him one more time. He wished for it the way he'd once yearned for the freedom to be his own person, to choose his own destiny.

Destiny, however, had just turned its back and was walking away.

Just as he was about to give up hope and tune in to Kyle, though, Lana turned and pinned him with a steady gaze.

A shot of warmth flooded through him and without thinking, he put the fork into his mouth, licking past the key lime pie to the last hint of Lana. She turned away then, and he spent the next half hour buzzing from the high.

She'd felt the pull, too. Which could only mean one thing.

Trouble. Pure trouble.

Chapter Five

The desert was dark and inviting, the perfect night to run. Lana stripped, then shifted just outside the guest house, needing the run badly. Anything to escape the feeling that heartbreak lurked behind every corner.

Little bits of cottonwood fluff stuck to her fur, tickling her nose as she ran ever higher and farther into the hills. She splashed across a thirsty creek and scrambled up a gully, then paused to shake out her fur. It was a glorious, full body shake that started at her nose and traveled all the way to the tip of her tail. What yoga did for her human body, a good shake did for her wolf.

She'd never felt this off-kilter before her arrival in Arizona. Make that since meeting Ty. The hum that had filled her ears in the dining hall was just an echo now, but it was still too loud to ignore. For years, she'd schooled her emotions, but now she was sliding off the edge of control—a feeling her wolf welcomed as much as her human side feared.

Her mind was spinning, her heart thumping. She felt alive, revived from a decade-long sleep. For the longest time, the only thing she'd felt any passion for was work, and she'd thrown herself into it. Submerged herself, even. Until now, she'd been too numb to feel like she'd missed anything.

But now, she wanted more. Life. Love. Passion.

All of it! her wolf cried.

It didn't matter that warning bells were clanging through the human part of her mind, telling her she was falling for a trick of the desert all over again. She'd felt exactly the same flicker of hope on her first visit to Arizona, only to leave bitter and broken-hearted. But since hope felt better than despair, she let her wolf take over. Let herself live, maybe even love.

She ran to the top of a rise, reveling in the power of her legs. To the east, parallel ribbons of red and white pulsed: the highway. In the foreground lay the muted lights of the ranch, half hidden behind sloping roofs. Over there was Jean's low duplex, the left half of which was now Nan's home. Everything was quiet, orderly, and apparently safe. But danger pressed in at the edges of the ranch; the world was full of it.

Her eyes jumped over a gap of darkness to an outlying house, an L-shaped adobe with wide windows and long, narrow skylights. Strips of tungsten light radiated between thick roof beams, glowing yellow against the indigo of the night. The way the house was perched at the far edge of the property suggested it might pick up and run clear into the desert if not for the split-log fence that surrounded it. She wondered who lived there, so far apart from the rest.

Then something stirred inside and —*click*— the lights went out. The house collapsed into brooding shadow as an owl hooted nearby. She cocked her head at the house. Who, who indeed?

She took off again, listening to her four paws scrape over the rocky ground in a steady tempo with the beating of her heart. On the next hilltop, she stopped, swung her head west and sniffed. There was something familiar out there in the wild. Something forbidden and oh-so tempting. She sniffed again, but just couldn't capture why this particular place, this rocky outcrop beside a spiky patch of cliffrose called to her. She turned a slow pirouette, taking in the princely view. She was flooded by the scent, the place, the memories.

The prickly tickle of sage, the smoky taste of mesquite, the fragrance of sycamore. Wrapping it all together like the curtain of night was a subtler scent that was unique and individual. Something piney, almost masculine.

She stopped short, then sniffed again, letting her nose peel back the layers in the air, one by one, until she'd dissected them right down to its essence—and froze in realization. Could it really be?

She swayed on her feet. The scent that drove her wild, that had stayed with her all these years—it wasn't the scent of the desert. It was Ty.

It was him, driving her crazy. Him, stirring her passion.

But how could that be? She searched her memories of her first visit to Arizona, years back. Somehow, she'd missed meeting Ty. Had he been away? One way or another, she'd caught his lingering scent. At that time, she'd put the intoxicating scent down to a trick of the desert and not an individual. But she'd been wrong. It was Ty.

For some reason, fate hadn't seen fit to deliver on that promise, all those years ago. All she'd been given then was a tiny hint, but it had been enough. In all the dark moments in the past twelve years, she'd cheered herself by imagining the desert: the space, the freedom, the sense of possibility. That crazy feeling of belonging.

No wonder her dreams were filled with red-rock mesas and vast, open spaces instead of the deep green woods of her home. No wonder the dry desert air soothed rather than scoured her throat. No wonder she'd never met a man who'd stirred her interest before. She'd been waiting for Ty without realizing it.

Ty, her destined mate.

The more she breathed in the view from this mesa high above the ranch, the more it made sense. As a shifter matured, so too did his scent. But that didn't mean the essence of it changed. It was like looking at a baby picture; the connection seemed so obvious once you linked the smooth features of the baby with the rugged adult.

That's what her instincts had been trying to tell her all along. He was her destined mate!

Far in the recesses of her mind, a voice warned that this was all much more complicated than it seemed. But she was in wolf form, and wolves had a way of simplifying things. He was hers, she was his.

Lana touched her nose to the cool earth and sniffed, delighted to find more traces of Ty. He'd spent time here, lots of it. His scent was everywhere, and it worked on her like a drug. She rolled on her back and wiggled, insisting it keep her company. Once, years ago, she'd had a similar feeling of something wonderful hanging just out of reach. Now it was just her and the stars and the same enchanted place, and for one moment, she let herself give in to it all and hope.

Hope? The human part of her mind wondered if she really dared.

∞∞∞∞

Ty flipped off the lights in his house, stepped outside, and shifted. When his body needed it most, the process was smooth, more thrilling than painful. When it was forced, shifting could be agony as cartilage stretched and bones realigned. Tonight the change from one body to the other was so seamless he barely noticed it. A moment later, his wolf gave a settling-in shake and took off at a hammering run.

By day, the desert slumbered, but at night, it pulsed with life. Cacti breathing, cereus blooming from the tips of their leaves. Birds and jackrabbits flitted from cover to cover, and even the hills seemed awake. He inhaled it with every weary breath. He knew every tussock and every stone, yet the desert's mood was different every night. There was always something hidden, unexpected.

A run was just what he needed after a hell of a day. Once he'd wrapped up business—to the extent that it could be wrapped up for the night—he had cleaned out the Jeep and discovered a torn luggage tag. Lana's. He'd sniffed the scrap, turned it over in his hands, and sniffed again. Even that little hint of her was intoxicating. Then he read the full name and address and froze.

Dixon. Lana Dixon. From the Berkshires, he remembered Aunt Jean saying.

Half the desert seemed to lodge in his throat at that moment of realization. Aunt Jean couldn't have been so bold as to invite one of *those* Dixons here, could she? He remembered his father cursing the name. If a Dixon ever tries to step foot here, *I'll kill him—or her.* His voice had been shaking as he said it, finger stabbing every word.

34

Lana was a Dixon? Here? It was pure insanity; his father wouldn't stand for it.

Except, of course, that his father wasn't home...yet. He'd be back in a week. Something in Ty's jaw twitched at the thought. Why would Jean act against his father's orders? And did Lana even know about the history between their families?

No, he decided. If she did, she would never have stepped foot on the ranch with that innocent, oblivious air.

He needed to run, to think. There were too many volcanoes rumbling, all of them threatening to erupt at once. The rogues. Lana and the shattering effect she had on him. The danger she had unknowingly wandered into. The mincemeat his father would make of him when he returned.

He gave his muzzle a vicious shake. A Dixon, back after all these years. Was it really possible?

He made a long, punishing loop to the west, then eased into a lope and turned north, making straight for his special place. The moon wasn't yet up, the stars all the brighter for its absence. Problems looked smaller from his hill. He knew it was an illusion, but hell, he needed a break like never before.

He pounded onto higher ground, past the last stands of thistle and the rambling barberry that marked his own private turf where no one dared disturb him. There, on the highest point of land, he looked east, beyond the slumbering valley. Any second now...

There. The rising moon. The globe was a few days short of full, but plump and heavy all the same. He could feel it singing through the earth even before the upper curve stole its first furtive glance over the ridge line. When the body followed, its pale light flipped a switch inside him. His rump hit the ground, his muzzle pointed up, and a low, rumbling cry left his muzzle. It rose, fell, then climbed again, bouncing off each undulation of the landscape. The desert was made for howling, lifting and amplifying the sound the way no other place could. He could howl all night, lose himself in the bittersweet ballad.

Lana—Lana Dixon—was here on the ranch. So near, so impossibly far. She was forbidden fruit, the Capulet to his Montague. The thought of what he would be denied gave him all the more reason to howl. He tipped his head back more and spilled his soul into the night. Hope, despair, and yearning, all tumbled together in his heart song.

Alone. He'd always be alone.

∞∞∞

Lana sensed the other wolf as a vague feeling even before she heard the measured breath of an athlete, the confident step of one at home. A shiver ran through the landscape at his approach, and everything hushed in anticipation. Then one of the shadows wavered and a wolf emerged from the darkness, heading to the highest outcrop a stone's throw away. She crouched, watching. The wind was with her; he hadn't caught her scent.

It was the most magnificent wolf she'd ever seen. Big. Taller than her by a head. His coat was a midnight shade of brown, like the strongest, most bitter coffee—no cream, no sugar, concentrated into a syrup you'd be crazy to sip, let alone swallow.

Ty, as bold and brooding in canine form as on two feet. A shudder of anticipation rolled through her.

The soft texture of his coat was framed by the harsh landscape, and power rolled off him like a heat wave. Frustration, too—mountains of it. When Ty tilted his head and howled, her heart stuttered. That bass was the voice of a prisoner, yearning to break free. Low and sorrowful, it swelled and modulated but never broke. She leaned into the night air, wanting to brush up against him, wanting to ease the unbearable loneliness.

In the next slow heartbeats, his voice seemed to grow louder, nearer. With a blink, she realized her wolf had taken up the cry too, and was pouring her soul into the night with him. The moon just yanked it out of her.

She pounded every aching minute of the past years into her howl and let the vast space multiply it a dozen times over. Ty's voice wavered as hers rose, and then broke off altogether. She wanted so badly for him to acknowledge the force that seemed to lasso them together, again and again. Destiny was at work here. Couldn't he tell?

She strained for some sign, but Ty didn't answer. She howled until her voice cracked on a last, echoing note, then let her head sink to the ground as silence crushed in around her. Maybe fate was playing an ever crueler trick this time, giving her a man who didn't love her back. She counted one hollow heartbeat, then another, feeling hope drain away. A tumbleweed hurried past; perhaps it, too, was chasing a reluctant mate.

That's when Ty started up again. She could have wept at the sound, half in joy, half in sorrow. She joined in on his next refrain, swelling with hope as their voices merged. The sound formed a bridge, and she could swear she felt his heart beat in her chest as their voices carried high and far. Their duet was a serenade, an incantation, urging the moon higher so that it might brighten the darkness and show them the way.

Every living thing stopped, listening in a reverent hush. Even the moon seemed to bend an ear. They struck their most perfect chord, and Lana hung on to it so long, so breathlessly, that she didn't notice when Ty stopped. Only that the night was still, except for his footfalls, drawing near.

She pulled in a sharp breath and trembled, fighting every instinct to drop her head in submission. Tonight, he wasn't the pack alpha. He was her mate.

Yes, her mate. Her wolf knew it and made damn sure any hesitation from her human side was firmly locked away.

God, he was big. Imposing. Proud. His eyes were bright and full of surprise at the female who refused to back away. She forced her tail to stay straight as a flag instead of letting it droop between her hind legs. If they were to be mates, they would do it on equal terms. She lifted her chin when he stopped, half a step away, the soft huff of his breath the only moving thing in the crisp night air.

When his muzzle went left, sniffing her space, hers mirrored the motion. When he swung right, she stayed in the middle. Let him look all he wanted. Let him come closer. Let him touch.

As if bidden, Ty stepped forward and did a slow lap of her body, his nose tracing an invisible boundary above her back, then breaking through it until he was brushing along her side. A spark crackled on her coat at his first contact, and her pulse started throbbing in her veins.

Mine! Mate!

Surely he knew it now, too?

Her heart thumped wildly as she leaned closer, pushing past the outer tips of his fur to feel the warmth beneath. He pulled slowly along the length of her left side and up to her face, then ran the underside of his chin over the nape of her neck in the ultimate wolf sign of trust. Much as she was tempted to roll and offer him her belly, she stood firmly on four feet. The daughter of an alpha could damn well hold her own, even if it meant hiding an inner tremble.

She started her own slow dance, running her muzzle up his neck and over his shoulder until they were intertwined, slow-wrestling for closer contact. She'd never felt warmth like this before—warmth that had her imagining the surrounding landscape lit with a thousand flickering candles set in irregular rows that turned the night into a place of worship. In a place like that, even the most jaded soul could find faith.

As Ty circled again, the inner throbbing grew more insistent. He paused at her rump, and this time, she dropped her haunches in a thinly veiled hint. She was ready for her mate. Burning for him, in fact. Instinct chanted within her, wanting him to mount, to slide inside, to give her pleasure like no lover ever before. Want became spoken need as she let out a low whine. Ty gave off an answering call, a rumble from deep within his chest that grew as he circled yet again and nuzzled her, face to face. He did it over and over, a gesture fit for a caring lover, not a mighty wolf who took what he wanted, as hard and fast as he wanted. It was she who was rushing, insisting. She couldn't help a little yowl, an insistent nudge of her hips.

Ty's rumble went deeper and she could sense a shiver of anticipation sweep through his body. His uneven breath and slow, almost reverent movements told her that this was different than the hundred ordinary conquests of a much-sought-after alpha.

She only intended to let out an encouraging yip, but she found herself in another heartfelt howl that begged the moon to shine the truth into Ty's eyes. A weight squeezed in beside her—Ty—and he howled too, underpinning her voice with his deeper harmony. She could picture a thousand moonlit nights spent in exactly this way. They'd let their voices wrap around each other, then let their bodies follow suit.

Every living thing in the desert stopped, listening to their song in a reverent hush. But just as they struck their most perfect chord, Ty's voice cut off in mid-cry.

A deathly quiet suffocated the hills, and her head snapped left to study Ty. In an instant, her mate had gone from singer to solid rock. His hackles were raised from nape to tail and his nose pointed at something—someone?—out in the shadows.

She tried to chisel some feature out of the darkness as a dozen mixed emotions coursed through her veins. Anger was foremost: anger at the trespasser who'd interrupted their serenade and made her mate an alpha again, protector of his pack. Awe came in a close second, because the power radiating off Ty was overwhelming. In the space of a heartbeat, he'd morphed from tender lover to king of the night. He stood stiff and tall, his only movement the flare of his nostrils and his bristling fur.

She sniffed the air. There was something out there, all right. Something distant and barely perceptible, like the pressure front at the leading edge of a desert storm. The hair along her spine spiked. Could it be the rogues?

When Ty shifted forward, she did the same. He took a step west, sniffing, then swung his head back to her with a quiet growl.

Go, his hard eyes said.

Their special moment was gone, and he wanted her gone so he could tend to the threat hovering in the night.

She took a defiant step forward. She would not be cowed. She would stand by him, not retreat. She would fight alongside him. She would—

Go. Now. That steely look was a direct order, alpha to subordinate.

Everything in her wanted to hate him at that moment. But instead of hating, her heart cracked wider open. Didn't he know he didn't have to face every enemy alone? Didn't he know she wanted to stand by his side?

His look didn't waver, and she had her answer. Duty came first with this man, duty above everything else.

Lana wanted to protest, but an order from an alpha was law, and she had no choice but to obey. It hurt, though, being brushed aside. Just like the frustrating days of her childhood, before she'd finally earned the right to fight alongside her brothers and make a stand for her pack.

But this wasn't her pack, not yet, anyway. Her shoulders turned away, and although her eyes tried to hang on to Ty, they, too were forced to join the retreat. She could practically hear the snakeweed snicker. Would this alpha ever respect her as an equal, or would he only see her as helpless and meek?

Lana didn't do helpless. She didn't know meek. She was a fighter, a leader in her own right.

Her human side bucked against his rejection. He didn't want her help? Well, she didn't want or need that kind of mate.

Her wolf, though, howled in protest, seeing a lifetime of regret ahead if she didn't act. *No! We can't give him up without a fight!*

They'd been so close to some great truth a moment ago. She could feel it. Finally her heart was waking up, like a seed that had been waiting for exactly the right conditions to germinate—and now this?

She gave her coat a violent shake, launching all but the most resolute burrs back into the scrub. Damned if she wasn't going to give her heart its due. Her stumble became a trot, her mind plotting as her paws padded over the cool ground. Tonight might not be the moment, but soon, she would find a way to win her mate. And if it ended in an excruciating crash and burn, well, at least she would know she'd tried.

Watch out, Alpha, she half-muttered as she slipped back toward the ranch. *Next time, I won't let you let me go.*

Chapter Six

For three days, Lana cast furtive glances around the ranch for Ty. The few times she spotted the alpha, he was silently smoldering or emitting his two-syllable version of speech. Even from a distance, she could feel the air shimmer and tense between them, but each time she sent a tentative thought his way, it hit a firewall. Shifters could usually sense one another's moods well, but Ty was unreadable. And if she got too close, he simply moved off in the opposite direction. Surely she hadn't been imagining the connection they'd made that night on the hill, so why was he avoiding her now?

A creeping doubt set in, telling her if she didn't act soon, she might lose her chance at her mate. But when to act, and how? She could hardly force the pack alpha to bend to her will.

Worse yet were the doubts. What if he never came around? What if he didn't want her? What if this was all just another cruel trick of destiny?

The one time she saw a woman touch Ty, her blood welled up so fast, she thought it might erupt out of her ears. It was Audrey again, that bleached blond who worked every inch of her voluptuous curves. The woman had the subtle social graces of a stripper. She didn't walk; she swung, working an invisible audience. When she laid a groping hand on Ty's forearm, every hair on Lana's neck went stiff. She barely held her wolf in check as Ty extracted himself and moved away. Audrey had watched him go with the look of a raptor eying its prey. Or was it a fox, plotting her next move? Either way, Lana decided to add Audrey to the list of dangers out here in the Wild West.

The rest of the pack members were friendly enough, though

busy in their own pursuits. That was fine with Lana; she was here to help her grandmother settle in, not to socialize. According to Jean, there were close to two hundred shifters on the ranch, many scattered across isolated parts of the vast property. Some of them worked the land, while the rest were involved in broader pack businesses that ranged across Central Arizona, from construction to consultancies and commercial real estate. Relations with their immediate neighbors were generally good, though a change in management over at the neighboring Seymour Ranch was the subject of concern, especially since an adjoining corner of that property had been deeded to the state as park land. The last thing the pack wanted was outsiders anywhere near their home.

"We could use someone like you, Lana!" Jean said as they hung pictures on day three.

They could, Lana knew. Back at home, she worked on land management issues, and the stakeholders she negotiated between were essentially the same as they were here: the pack, the public, commercial interests, and environmental lobbyists. So, yes, she could bring a lot of experience to Twin Moon Ranch.

If she wanted to stay.

One sniff of the desert air reminded Lana just why she should, and just why she shouldn't.

She changed the subject quickly. "How real is this rogue threat?"

"I'm sure Ty has it under control," Jean said with forced calm.

She held back a snort. The only way to control a rogue was a fight to the death, and from the sound of it, there were several on the prowl. Would it come to that? She had to admit that she itched to fight, to act. Anything to ease the tension in the air.

More than that, she itched with a desperate need to connect with Ty. That need wasn't just rooted in her heart or mind; it was hard-wired into her soul, and her whole being ached with it. For years, she'd been telling herself that a broken heart was as bad as it got, but now she was thinking that a functioning one was even worse. *Ty, Ty, Ty.* His name was a chant in her blood, and it pulsed through every part of her body, day and night.

She'd tried running off her frustration after dark, but found only temporary relief. The minute she stopped moving and shifted back to her human form, she would lie in bed burning from her own heat. Using her fingers on herself provided only the slightest bit of the release she craved. It worked if she imagined Ty's hands gliding over her body and sliding into her core, imagined that it was his weight pressing down on her instead of emptiness. But afterwards, she was just as heated and empty as before.

"How are you doing, sweetie?" Nan asked, pulling her attention back to the house.

"Fine, fine," Lana lied between hammer blows to a nail on the wall where her grandmother wanted a picture.

"Enjoying the ranch?"

Lana pinched the next nail between her lips and made as neutral a sound as she could, then gave the first nail another couple of murderous hits. She'd be enjoying the ranch a hell of a lot more if Ty would stop avoiding her.

She tried to shake the feeling off, but it was as deeply rooted as the porcupine quills she'd seen lodged in the muzzle of a miserable-looking ranch dog. That was her: a stupid mutt. If only someone would come along with a pair of pliers and yank the heartache out of her.

Surely her happiness didn't depend on one man, let alone a bossy alpha. *You can damn well function without a man.*

Her wolf snarled. *Not without this one!*

The beast was getting more and more difficult to control. Lana didn't want to think what would happen when the waxing moon filled. Would she chase Ty to the ends of the Earth or do the smart thing: run the hell away?

She paced, muttered, and endured for three aching days and two torturous nights, until the night of the full moon.

∞∞∞∞

43

The moon wasn't just full; it was painfully full. Bloated, even. Lana slipped out of the suffocating adobe bungalow and shifted, wondering what the night would bring.

Her wolf was eager to get out and run. Too eager, maybe, but the beast wouldn't be denied. So she loped out past the circle of light that defined the inner ranch and into the pale black-and-white world that was the desert at night. She sniffed in the direction of Ty's hill, but there was no fresh trail pulling her that way. Instead, she ranged south and west and found herself heading toward the corner where pack land met Seymour Ranch property. When a truck rattled past on the dirt road below, she ducked behind a spindly bush and tucked in her tail. Who was in such a hurry at this time of night?

She followed in a crouched run for a good mile before the truck came to stop beside two others. One vehicle on these roads was normal. Two might be called a conference. But three? Something was definitely wrong. She squinted into the crescent of headlights. Her breath hitched when she spotted Ty stepping out of the truck. Cody seemed to have arrived first, and the brothers locked gazes just long enough to mentally communicate some urgent message.

Three other men stood to the side, spitting angry looks. They converged with Ty and Cody and created one seething huddle. Even from a distance, she could tell Cody was trying to keep things calm. Ty, on the other hand, was a picture of barely controlled fury. The other three were rifle-toting humans who looked all too itchy to shoot.

She crept forward, keeping to the shadows. Her nose wrinkled, catching the unmistakable scent of coagulated blood and bloated flesh. A morbid kind of curiosity drew her onward. What—or who—had died here?

Another careful step, and she had the answer. Dead sheep. She could make out the carcasses now, three or four of them tossed about a slope. They'd been shredded alive by some animal bent on destruction. She crept closer and sniffed again, then pulled her head back at the tell-tale acid scent of rogues.

They must have come and gone hours ago, but they were sure to strike again. Somewhere, sometime. Soon.

44

Except the smell was too overpowering to come from just a couple of sheep. She crouched lower, letting the fur of her belly brush the ground as she crept forward to peer over a rise. Clumps of desert scrub shifted and waved in the slight breeze. Among them were softer, rounder heaps that didn't stir at all. She drew back at the sight of more dead sheep. Many more. Her eyes made out the brand on the nearest body—a double S—and her mind spun. Clearly, the three humans from Seymour Ranch hadn't seen the extent of the carnage. Once they did, they'd kick up a fuss from here to the state capital. An investigation would ensue, and the pack's fragile anonymity would be threatened.

She had to help distract them. Cody and Ty were still talking to the men, obviously trying to draw them away from the hollow where the majority of the sheep lay. A diversion, that's what they needed. But what? She glanced around, wondering if she could set off a rock slide or let out a howl. No, it would be foolish to appear in wolf form here. They'd blame her for the massacre. What then?

The three humans were already pushing past Cody and moving toward the side of the road. In another minute, they would discover the rest of the sheep and all hell would break loose. Without giving much thought to her plan, she shifted back to her human form, her mind was spinning with a single thought.

Fast. She had to act fast.

∞∞∞∞

Ty stopped just short of yanking the Seymour ranchers back from the edge of the road. So they were angry—so what? He personally had leapfrogged anger and gone straight to fury.

Yas was responsible for this carnage. He knew it. Clearly, the rogue was back with a band of troublemakers and was once again trying to pit humans against wolves in the hope that they'd kill each other off. The Seymour Ranch hands would set off a massive wolf hunt, which in turn would rile up his fellow shifters. Sooner or later, things would escalate. All it took was one of his cockier packmates to shift in plain view of a human, and the pack's true nature would be exposed.

Ty shook his head, keeping his wolf shackled inside. Didn't Yas realize that trouble for the wolf pack would eventually extend to his own brethren?

Right. Like rogues were capable of thinking that far ahead or that clearly.

The last few days had been agonizing even without the threat of rogues. He had taken to running night patrols just to keep his mind off Lana. Whenever he let himself get too close to her, he was squeezed in a vice between duty and overwhelming desire. Too far, and his wolf strained at a rapidly fraying leash.

All week, he'd struggled to find a solution. Somehow, he had to lock out emotion and get on with his life. Above all, he had to get Lana to safety, even if it meant denying himself. There were too many dangers for her here. He could tick them off on three fingers: one, the rogues. Two, his father. Three, himself. Because what if that humming force started up between them again? He'd never be able to resist, and it wouldn't end well for her, just as it hadn't ended well for his mother, or any of his father's women.

A seductive voice whispered in the back of his mind. *Unless she's your true mate.*

When Lana joined in on his howling a few nights back, something inside him had swelled and nearly burst past his self-imposed boundaries. He would have howled into sunrise with her if not for the rogues. In mid-howl, though, he'd caught a murmur deep in the night. It was barely there, more of a portent than a presence. But it had been enough to shatter the magic and tear him away.

But maybe that had been for the best. He'd almost forgotten she was a Dixon that night.

He'd been on his way to check out the threat when he was called back to the ranch by another report of rogue activity that turned out to be a false alarm. He cursed himself. If he had followed his first hunch, the trouble would never have gone this far.

He blinked, focusing on the present. Right now, he had to stop the ranchers before they discovered the other sheep. Then he could call out his trackers and chase the rogues all the way to hell.

A scream pierced the night air and he spun toward it, along with Cody and the humans. When a figure came crashing through the brush, the ranchers surged forward, rifles raised.

"Help!" A desperate voice cried out. "Help!"

The ranchers stepped back when a woman stumbled onto the road, and every muscle in his body cramped. It was Lana, crying and flailing and naked as the day she was born. Beautiful, every inch of her, even in hysteria. She threw herself at Dale, the Seymour ranch foreman, capturing him in a terrified embrace. "I was, I was—" she stuttered, pawing the man. Dale stood in shock, trying to prop her up without touching too much naked flesh.

Ty's blood massed in great clumps, then surged forward in dam-bursting floods. Like hell he would let any other man see her—touch her! He strode over in three steps, unbuttoned his flannel shirt, and draped it around Lana like a cape. She continued to babble as he pulled her away, something about a man and a prank and a truck and—

She winked. In the middle of it all, Lana winked at him. He nearly pulled up in surprise, though she kept babbling away and clutching his T-shirt, acting all the world like a woman frightened half out of her mind.

Acting? What the hell was she up to?

He caught Cody's eyes, which were twinkling with some inside joke Ty just couldn't catch. What was so funny here?

Whatever her game was, it was working. The ranchers' eyes were glued to this damsel in distress, torn between wanting to comfort her and getting a better view of her gloriously fit ass. He maneuvered her to the far side of his truck, glad only for the fact that no one made a move toward the rise. The sheep were forgotten, at least for the moment.

That's when his mind finally made sense of Lana's wink. She'd created a diversion, just in time.

"I don't know if I should kill you or kiss you," he muttered, then snapped his mouth shut.

Lana grinned from ear to ear. "Kiss," she whispered, letting her lips brush his ear.

One little word had never sounded so dangerous or delicious. The hiss of it stayed in his ear and shot straight into his bloodstream.

Kiss, the wolf in him purred.

Kill, the man thought in half-hearted resistance.

He didn't dare open his mouth for fear of which word might come out. A good thing Cody was on the ball, convincing the ranchers that he and Ty would deal with the situation.

"Enough for one night," he suggested, his voice working its usual magic. Even through the glare of his anger, Ty couldn't help wishing he had his brother's gift with words. "We'll take care of this," Cody cooed to the Seymour ranch hands. "We'll find the coyote responsible. We'll take care of him."

It was a miracle he could hear anything through the roaring in his ears. Damn it! She was so close. He tried prying Lana away, keeping her at arm's length to somehow hold on to his sanity. But his mind and his muscles found themselves at odds, and the heat of her stayed right against his ribs.

The ranchers muttered half-heartedly but they fired up their pick-up and drove away. Ty caught Cody's chuckle when Lana abruptly stopped raving, straightened, and gave them a pert nod. She was—laughing?

He could have throttled them both. "Get in the truck," he growled.

Lana crossed her arms and dug her bare heels into the ground.

He worked his jaw so hard it emitted a sharp crack. "Get in the truck, *please*."

Lana let a stubborn moment tick by, then climbed into the truck, slamming the door for good measure.

"I'll take care of this," Cody said, waving toward the sheep. "You go take care of... that." He motioned toward the truck and turned away with a badly disguised smile.

Rogue coyotes, human neighbors who'd come within a hair of discovering a terrible secret, and a hard-headed woman who had the gall to assume he needed help. A Dixon, no less. And those two were laughing?

Not only that, but crap, the night was still young.

∞∞∞

He drove in silence, unable to summon a word as Lana's tempting scent filled the cab. It was even more striking than the day he'd brought her up from the airport. Tonight, her scent was bold, lusty. Downright provocative. He rolled down the windows and tried breathing through his mouth.

With a grunt, he finally gave in and smacked the steering wheel. "Damn it! What were you thinking, bursting in naked back there?"

Lana crossed her arms over the flannel shirt—*his* flannel shirt, meaning their scents were mingling far, far too suggestively—and stared at him in silent challenge.

"Those men... everyone saw you!"

She arched an eyebrow, and something wild glowed in her blue eyes. *So did you,* purred her wolf. *And what did you think?*

A sudden flash of hot hammered his body. *We like, we like!* His wolf growled. He tightened his fingers around the steering wheel lest they reach out to stroke her silky hair.

"You have to admit it worked." She looked smug.

If hardening every cock on the scene was her goal, then yes, it had certainly worked. Because his was still erect and straining at his jeans. He held his tongue before it licked her all over, starting with that sassy mouth and ending in another warm, wet cavity.

The thought only hardened the bulge in his jeans. He couldn't remember ever getting as quickly—or as desperately—aroused by a woman. Fury spearheaded the stampede, with jealousy and desire not far behind. There was something else, too, trembling all the way in the back. Fear? His back went stiff. What did he have to be afraid of?

One glance at her freckled nose told him what. He could lose himself in her, forget who he was and what his duties were. Forget who she was. No way could he fraternize with the daughter of his father's sworn enemy.

Lana watched the funnel of light thrown by the truck's high beams. "Look, I was out for a run when I came across you guys. They were about to see the rest of the sheep. So I did the first thing I could think of to distract them."

"You succeeded," he agreed, squeezing the wheel harder at the thought of all those men, raking her body with their eyes. And her hands had been all over Dale! Ty couldn't have wrapped his shirt around her fast enough, and when he did, the contact was electrifying. All he'd wanted to do was smooth the cloth over every curve of her body.

Another heavy pause pinched the air.

"You're not mad, are you?" Her voice cracked slightly.

Mad? He was furious! He was beside himself! He was... he was melting fast, going all soft and mushy inside while his groin was still rock hard. Desperate to touch her, taste her— and that was just the beginning of his list. He sniffed the air and found it thick with her lust. His was there, too, weaving itself around hers. Jesus, the temptation.

Lana leaned toward him, her eyes closed, chin tilted up. Her expression went from inquisitive to warm as she cracked into a satisfied smile at his scent. Her eyes opened and landed right on his. Eyes that were more wolf than human. *Gotcha*, they said. On the heels of that came an open invitation. *I want you, wolf.*

He whipped his eyes to the road, jerking the truck back from a swerve that kicked up a shower of giggling gravel.

"Gotta love the night air," Lana said, refolding the unbuttoned shirt over her torso and tossing her long hair. She had no idea how much he wanted to tangle his fingers in there and pull her to him. She had no idea how bad it would be if he allowed that to happen. The air crackled with the energy of a whip, poised to snap.

As the truck reached the crest of a hill, his traitorous foot eased off the gas pedal. In the rear view mirror, the red tail lights of the rancher's vehicles were mere fireflies in the landscape. Cody's vehicle was still back there, headlights pointing into the brush.

He killed the engine but left his hand on the wheel, closing his eyes. Lana was waiting for him, toying with his heart. It was torture, sheer torture. Didn't she realize why they couldn't be together?

No, he realized. She didn't.

"Lana," he started, mustering all his self-discipline. Her name nearly stuck on his teeth. His tongue wanted to keep it there and roll it around. "Lana, your father is Nate Dixon."

Her eyes narrowed. "So?"

He waited, hoping the night would do the telling for him. "No one ever told you?"

"Told me what?"

He scrubbed a hand across his jaw. "Your parents used to live here in Arizona. You know why they left?"

She crossed her arms over the flannel. "They wanted a new start out East, so they went back to my dad's home pack."

So that's what they'd told her. A grain of truth buried at the heart of the lie. Nate Dixon did hail from back East. He'd come to Arizona to try something new and worked his way up the hierarchy of a struggling new pack, alongside Ty's father. The two had been best friends until they fell for the same woman.

"What about your mother?" he asked.

"What about my mother?" Lana's hands balled into fists.

"They didn't mention who she was with before she met your father?"

"What does that have to do with anything?"

She wasn't getting it. His fingers drummed the dashboard as he wondered how to say it. Finally, he drew in a deep breath and began. "Your mother was with my father. But she left him when she got pregnant—by Nate Dixon."

Chapter Seven

"My mother? Your father? Never." She spat the words out, clenching a fist in her lap.

Ty knew better than to answer that one. At least Lana seemed angrier with the situation than at him. He wanted to reach out and touch her, to somehow make it all right. But he was powerless.

It was torture, being this close to her, just as it was torture to think about the blood that ran through his veins. He admired his father as an alpha, but the man was a heartless bastard. He'd knocked up Ty's mother, then gone off and seduced Lana's mother. Not that he'd loved either woman. That was the crazy part. The blood feud was based entirely on the old man's hurt pride.

When Lana's mother left—in a hurry, no doubt—with Dixon, Ty's father took his mother back just long enough to knock her up a second time. The tortured woman had stuck around one more year before running away, abandoning Ty and his sister. Ty closed his eyes at his vague memories of a dark-haired woman with sad eyes. He could still taste the salt of her tears, hear her sobs as she hugged him goodbye. But he couldn't blame her for leaving. Not after the way his dad treated her.

Another woman had promptly filled her place in his father's bed, if not in Ty's heart. Cody's mother. Then she, too, left, her haunted eyes filled with shattered dreams. It was a cycle that had repeated itself, again and again. A cycle that Ty, the oldest child, observed as a mute witness.

He gripped the wheel so hard, the leather started to tear under his nails. His father's blood ran in his veins and though it gave him strength, it also doomed him to a lonely existence. But it was better to be alone than to be proven a bastard like his father. If only the pack females could accept that instead of trying to twist the occasional night of fun into something more, trying to land what they saw as a prize. He snorted. Some prize he'd be.

At least, that's what he thought before the phantom came along to tease him. For a time, he'd let himself believe there was someone out there strong enough to be his mate. It was the same now that Lana was here. That vision of a better life was back, tapping inside his skull, begging for him to open the door. He'd been so sure the phantom was his intended mate that he vowed never to lose his heart again. Yet here he was, doing it all over for another woman. If that didn't prove he was a faithless bastard like his father, what did?

His eyes did their best to focus on a saltbush just outside the truck. It would be awfully satisfying to watch it burst into flames. From the hot feel of his eyes, that might not be far off.

Lana was shaking her head, maybe reconsidering that held-back punch. He wished she'd just sock him. It would make him feel better. Her, too. Why did they both have to be masters of self-restraint?

Then something in her countenance changed. She looked softer, her eyes focusing just left of his face. On his ear. He jerked his hand back to the steering wheel. So he'd been scratching again. Okay, more like clawing. No big deal.

The storm in her eyes dissipated, replaced by puffy cumulus clouds. She looked...sympathetic. At least one chamber of his heart misfired before limping on with the rest.

"Our parents don't have anything to do with us, Ty."

"They have everything to do with us. My father put a death threat out on yours."

"So?"

So? "That extends to all Dixons. Including you. You shouldn't...you can't be here."

Lana threw her hands up in the air. "Then why would I be allowed to come out here?"

"I'm guessing Jean didn't exactly mention who'd be coming to visit. And your grandmother, too. She must have known."

"Why wouldn't Nan be banished, too?"

He shrugged. "She's a generation older. Not her fault what her daughter did. I mean, that's the way he'd see it. I just can't believe she'd risk bringing you out here. Why would she do that?"

Lana let out a stuttering breath. "Good old Nan. Always had her own way of doing things."

He refrained from adding something about the apple not falling far from the tree. "Lana, we can't pretend there is no feud."

She spun around to face him. "We can't pretend there is no *this*," she insisted, fanning the energized air between them.

He shut his eyes and pressed his foot even harder against the brake pedal, as if that might stop her scent from getting the better of him. He wanted her. She wanted him. They'd both been smoldering for days. But this was one fire that could never be permitted to blaze.

In a last act of resistance, he shoved the truck door open so hard it bounced back against its hinges. He pushed it again and heaved himself out into the night, sucking in the cool air. The slam of the door behind him flattened the hushed landscape, and even the wind hurried away. He took three brisk steps, realized there was no escape, and stopped, hanging his head.

How many times had he cursed being his father's son? Always having to be the best, not permitted to be like the others. But none of the expectations, none of the foregone conclusions as to who he was and what he would someday be—none of that was as bad as this. The gavel had already been slammed on their case. Whatever there was between him and Lana, it simply wasn't allowed to exist.

The sole of his left foot found a small rock and rolled it over and back, kneading it into the ground as he contemplated his fate. Maybe if he worked it long enough, he could grind the thing into dust.

Why Lana? Why now? He didn't understand it. All he knew was that she was incredible. Tough and spunky, ballsy and beautiful. What wasn't there to love?

The rolling stone stuttered as he slammed the brakes on his thoughts. Who'd said anything about love? Just because he wanted to take a dip inside her didn't mean he wanted her permanently. He was alpha! He had a job to do. He couldn't let anything impinge on his duty to the pack.

There. Just another reason he couldn't have Lana.

Damn but his ear was itchy tonight. He wanted to scratch the whole of it away with the thickest, thorniest branch he could find. He could start with his ear, then go on to the rest of his body, because the itch was all-consuming.

A creak sounded behind him, followed by a gentle thump as the passenger door opened and closed. Pebbles crunched, signaling Lana's movement around the truck. His canines surged against his gums. He'd have to fight himself on this one. The feud was almost a moot point. If he took her, she'd wilt away, like all his father's women had done.

She can handle it, his wolf insisted. *She's the one.*

He shook his head. *We'd empty her. Maybe even kill her.*

She looked us straight in the eye. She can do it!

Even if she could, we'll only let her down.

Never! his wolf screamed.

"Ty." Lana's voice slipped through the crisp night air, low and viscous. He wished he could let that honey soothe his throat and free everything shackled inside.

He knew he shouldn't let her close, but for the first time in his life, he was frozen by a whole host of fears that confronted him at the same time. The fear of failure—what if he couldn't control himself? Fear of consequences—for her. As for himself, he was already damned.

He closed his eyes. She was only an inch in front of him now. All he needed to do was reach out an arm and tug her flush against his body, and this desperate itch would be soothed.

"Need a little fresh air?" Lana teased. The gleam in her eye made it perfectly clear: her wolf had taken over.

He suppressed a growl. "Need a little of you." The words popped out through clenched teeth. He winced, knowing she wasn't the only one having trouble controlling the wolf within.

His hands clutched at his pockets, afraid where they might go if allowed to roam free.

Her fingers brushed the line of his jaw before coming to rest on his chest, and his body hummed like a musical instrument plucked, then left to vibrate.

"Need a lot of you." Lana stretched onto her toes and pressed her lips to his. They were soft, wet, perfectly sculpted to his. And they were driving him wild—both man and wolf.

On the outside, he barely flinched. He couldn't— wouldn't—let this happen! Even if she was reckless enough to push them both over the edge, he would resist. He lifted his hands intending to push away, but somehow, they cupped her waist instead. He huffed out half a curse. Was his mind the only one here who understood something about consequences?

Lana kissed his ear and fondled his collar, making his head angle closer. She was picking at one side of his inner lock while his wolf was scratching madly at the other. Between the two of them, he was a goner.

Need a lot of you. Either she whispered it again or the words were still ricocheting through his mind.

She cozied up to him as though she'd done it a hundred times before. It felt so familiar, so right. "I want you hard and fast," she whispered, nosing the curves of his ear. "I want you wet and wild." His cock bobbed in agreement as her lips traced the line of his jaw. Her voice echoed through his head as she went on, breaking straight into his fantasies. "Then I want you slow and sensual."

His wolf seized onto the words with a lusty howl. Yes, his wolf had a very clear vision of how he wanted her, and when and where. Like right here. Right now. Consequences be damned.

He managed a low grumble despite the roaring in his ears. "Slow and... what?"

She drew the word out, weaving her fingers through his hair. "Sen-su-al."

"Sensual," he repeated, drawing it out. The whole language of this night felt foreign. The irresistible pull toward Lana, the humming in his veins. Everything about it gave him a thrill, especially now that her hand was wandering south. Part of his mind still sputtered excuses. How would he ever explain slow and sensual to his father? What would he say to the tribunal that would be assembled to lynch them both once they were discovered?

Lana hadn't buttoned the shirt and it flapped wide, the fabric brushing his thigh. He felt her take his left hand, circle his palm with her thumb, and press it to the soft flesh of her breast. Warm and supple, it echoed the rise and fall of her lungs. He held his breath, trying to beat back the tidal wave about to sweep him away.

"To hell with everyone else," she whispered, letting her long, toned body melt onto his. They were a perfect match, two continents lining up after eons of separation.

Mine! his wolf roared, lips already reaching for hers.

∞∞∞∞

Lana's human side knew she should stop, but her wolf just wouldn't let go. There was no way to resist this irrepressible force, not even if she wanted to.

Ty wore the expression of a boy holding the key to a lion's cage, terrified of the beast he was about to set free. His shoulders were tense, his eyes smoldering.

Maybe she wasn't the only one who'd been living through a drought these last years.

Her nipples hardened as she leaned into him and his lips finally yielded to hers. Slow and delicious, that's what this was. Her blood swelled as her pulse quickened. It was the first time her heart had ever asked—begged—for anything, and suddenly, she wanted it all.

Finally, he was hers. His eyes were a warm drink, something to sip and enjoy. His lips cried out his need for her. His tongue ventured deeper and everything exploded from there.

One second, she was thinking *nice* as he gently sampled her lips. The next, his callused hands clamped over her flanks and his mouth ravaged hers.

First up on the program, hard and fast.

A blink later, he had her up against the truck, clutching her left leg to his waist. She went on tippy toe with the right until Ty lifted it, wrapping both of her legs around him. She heard herself groaning, pressing her folds against his naked flesh where his shirt had pulled up, burning for more contact. Growling into his ear as he dipped his head and simultaneously slid one of his hands up from her waist. Lips and fingers met at a nipple and began to tease. The man was walking steel, yet his touch was zephyr light.

"We can't do this," he whispered. The rest of him, though, seemed all in.

The chafe of his stubble against her sensitive flesh set her soul singing. "We need to do this," she insisted, pushing her hips against his. No way would her wolf let him get away this time.

She held on as the tension battered him like an ocean wave, until piece by piece, the stubborn scraps of resistance broke down and washed away. Satisfaction washed through her, because this rock of a man was melting—for her. When she arched her back, Ty responded by kneading her nipple with enough passion to drive all logic straight out of her mind. There was no way she could think now, not with him touching her that way. Not with him... carrying her?

She clung to him, eyes fluttering over a shifting landscape of swaying alders, ragged mesquite, and solid rock. Or maybe the latter was Ty. He could be dragging her off to a cave for all she cared. Everything in her screamed for fulfillment.

There was a creak, then a metallic groan as Ty opened the truck's tailgate and tipped her back with a sure hand. The night sky stretched out as far as she could see, forming a boundless panorama with Ty in the foreground. She lifted her head, eager to watch him strip and slide into her. But his hands stayed on her hips, aligning her with the edge of the gate, too high for his waist. What was he doing?

His hands reached back for her ankle. "Up," he rasped, patting his shoulder.

A shiver ran through her as she realized what he intended. It was one thing for a wolf's tongue to explore a lover's groin, but the act seemed too intimate for casual human coupling. She'd always shied away from giving men access to that part of her, at least with their tongues.

Until now. Nothing was too intimate with Ty. Her pulse raced as she lifted both legs to his shoulders and let her knees buckle, not just opening the curtains but hauling back the entire theater walls. She was handing herself to a near stranger on a silver platter, possessed by some outside force. Yet it felt good. More than good. Liberating.

She couldn't think beyond that, not with his finger parting her folds. All she knew was that this was an experience beyond any she'd had before, the kind she thought could only exist in her dreams. Her mind just managed to link together that train of thought before his glowing eyes met hers, and he lowered his head to her core.

At the touch of his tongue, her vision exploded into the fiery trails of a hundred comets. Ty lapped at her, first slowly, then with greed, exploring every millimeter of her hidden flesh. She could feel him inhaling her scent, hovering like an intoxicated hummingbird at her entrance, then drinking his fill of her sweet nectar.

She wanted to hum in return. Hell, to sing, to prance with joy. Somehow, hard and fast had gotten mixed up with wet and wild, and the result was better than her hottest fantasies. Because she wasn't just wet; she was dripping. Feeling ridiculously delicious. She wound her fingers in his hair, riding a rushing wave as his tongue zeroed in on her bud and explored. Meanwhile, one finger, then another slipped deep into her, eliciting a juicy rush and a moan as her muscles clenched around him. She gyrated under him on the brink of letting go.

Ty pulled back for long enough to fix her with his glowing gaze. "Okay?" His voice was husky.

She could barely nod in response. Was there a word for how she felt? Not in any language she knew. Ty's lips curled into the slightest of smiles. She moaned as he dipped back for more. Words tapped at the boundary of her mind, and she was sure she could read his thoughts. *I am going to push you right over the edge, woman.*

Ha, she thought vaguely. *I'm already there.*

Then I will catch you in mid-fall, he grunted, *and start all over again.*

She lost herself in a searing rush of pleasure, and Ty's name ground past her lips as his fingers stirred faster. Then he paused abruptly, teasing for one whispering second before rushing back in with a flick of the tongue, pushing her over the edge. She cried out long and loud, clinging to her high even as it slipped slowly back into the night.

∞∞∞∞

The weight of Ty's head on her stomach anchored Lana in place and time, guiding her gently back to Earth.

Over here, she heard the warmth of his body calling. *Over here.*

Nowhere else I want to be, she called back in her mind.

The way he'd gone right to the mark made her wonder if they'd been lovers in a past life. How else could Ty know her so well? Or maybe that was just the way of destined mates. Her fingers played along his shoulders as the breeze carried his earthy scent to her. It was interlaced with hers now, thick with desire.

She sighed in sheer pleasure. Never had letting go felt so good. Never had she felt so sure in her defiance. She looked up at the stars, and they smiled back in reassurance. No, this couldn't be wrong.

Ty's broad mass stirred against her stomach, stoking her desire once more. A shiver went through her, making Ty lift his head with an inquiring gaze. That look—and the promise in it—sent cubes of ice skating down her spine. Ty misinterpreted her reaction and eased the flaps of her shirt down, keeping her warm. He looked like he was about to pull off his T-shirt when he stopped and hopped into the bed of the truck in one smooth move instead. She scooted out of the way as Ty pulled a blanket from a corner and spread it over the truck bed.

"Just an old horse blanket," he muttered, shaking his head.

"I'd be fine lying on a bed of nails," she murmured, settling back onto it, her hands resting lightly on her lower ribs, the shirt wide open. "As long as you're with me." Amazing, she thought, that she could say it without blushing. She'd never uttered those words to a man before. Never would again—not to any man but him.

Ty leaned down for a kiss that she never wanted to end, then pulled away and stood. He yanked his shirt off in one determined sweep, exposing a rippled expanse of neatly stacked muscle. A thin trail of hair started around his navel and disappeared suggestively into his jeans.

She gulped. That trail, she would be happy to follow.

He lowered the shirt to her outstretched hand and watched her ball it under her head. A slow, sultry grin spread across his face. An actual smile that offered the slightest hint of the boy Aunt Jean had referred to.

She stretched her arms, reaching up toward the winking stars. A little farther and she'd grab the tail of Scorpio and slingshot into space.

"My legs are freezing," she cooed, sliding her calf along his. "Covered in goosebumps." Never mind that they had nothing to do with the cold. Lana held her next breath, watching Ty pop the button of his jeans, slide the zipper, and let his hand snake inside. She sucked in a long, aching breath. Now he was teasing her. The nerve!

Mine! She tugged at the cuff of his jeans until he gave in, sliding both hands down to shuck his pants and boxers. His glowing eyes looked down on her from six feet above, forming a new constellation: the wolf. The very erect wolf. Even the chirping cicadas seemed to take note, singing a lusty chorus into the night.

His eyes raked her body as he stroked his own shaft to perfection, taking his time. Was he imagining her doing that to him? She watched, rapt. His cock twitched as she rolled the flannel off her shoulders and pushed it aside. The fiery glow in his eyes radiated power, but when his gaze reached her, all she felt was the soft touch of candlelight. She could swim in that feeling—that warm, safe place she wanted to stay in forever.

When Ty folded his magnificent body and came down to all fours over her aching frame, she came undone. Her arms stretched over her head, her back arched, and her knees fell to the sides—all before he'd even touched her. Then he intertwined his fingers with hers and squeezed a promise. *I will love you, woman,* his touch said, *like I've never loved anyone before.*

Chapter Eight

Ty stopped thinking and gave himself over to the sweet sensation enveloping him. Duty had fallen to desire; his restraint was shredded to tatters. But try as he might, he just couldn't summon any guilt. Lana was his. Every fiery touch, every flutter of his heart said so.

Just lying on Lana's stomach after tasting her gave him a high. The feel of her chest rising and falling let him sink comfortably toward whatever end fate had in store for them. He all but hummed at the gentle play of her fingers across his back, tracing the occasional scar. Thirty seconds, he'd given her. Truth be told, he needed it, too. Thirty seconds to absorb the rich taste of her and collect the scattered pieces of his mind.

He met her eyes and marveled at the way she held his gaze, telegraphing her need. He knew the danger in his eyes intensified when he was aroused—whether in anger or in passion. Every lover he'd ever taken had kept her eyes firmly shut, her soul locked away. But Lana's sky blues were wide open and utterly at ease. More than that, they looked at him with wonder and promise. The promise of more than a single night, of more than just physical pleasure.

I told you so, his wolf chided. *She can take it. She can withstand the fire in our eyes.*

He hoped to hell it was true, because he couldn't hold back any more.

He wanted to draw out this peaceful moment—for her and for himself—but Lana's nipples were straining for his lips. He could almost taste them. When he finally took one in his mouth, she gasped, and his cock grew harder still. His lips curved into a satisfied smile even as they continued to tease her. When had he ever been so fascinated by a woman's reaction to his touch? Never. But then again, he'd never known a woman like this.

Never. He already knew that word would get a lot of use tonight.

With one hand intertwined with her fingers and the other beside her head, he felt long, light, and powerful. She had power, too, albeit a more subtle kind. Her abdomen was rippling seductively under him, her hips climbing, forcing contact. The heat building in him spiked again.

All too often, his packmates tiptoed around him, measuring their every word, every gesture. Lana was refreshingly direct, honest. Unintimidated.

And now, she was unraveling at his touch. A satisfied rumble built in his chest. His inner wolf was damned pleased with what he saw. He'd given her a climax to end all climaxes, and now he would deliver another, and another, setting a new standard each time.

One push of his hips, and his cock plunged in so swiftly, so easily, that he nearly lost his balance. Like they were made for each other. Her inner muscles drew wide to accommodate him, then clenched tight around him. She was all there, all his, just as he was all hers. Amazing how comfortably that idea sat on his shoulders.

He withdrew, teasing her entrance, then slid back in, thrilled as much by her moan as the pulsing sensation inside her. On his next withdrawal, she pressed up, rolling him over. He found himself on his back, blinking at the stars while Lana hovered over him with a wicked look. *Can you handle this, alpha? Can you handle me?*

He was about to roll back and retort something about being able, but not willing when—*Whoa.* His train of thought was cut short as she flipped her hair back and balanced over the length of his cock.

Okay, he might just be willing to humor her, if only for a short time.

Lana shifted her hips and slowly, deliciously slid over his hard length. He let his eyes close and a low groan escape his throat. His hands shifted to her hips and ground them closer. She slid off and back on a second time, then a throbbing third. When his eyes cracked open, they found Lana's half-closed in concentration. She mouthed his name, then cartwheeled her arms and leaned back in a graceful arc that lifted and stretched her breasts as she angled into him. The sight of her nipples, front and center, stirred a new chord in him. Small but supple, swollen with need, her breasts swayed as she continued to roll her hips. Her liquid core drew him deeper and deeper as she fought back throaty groans of delight. That alone did him in, stirring a new chord of desire.

He slid this thumb along the sinew of her hip until it nudged her clit, watching for her reaction. There. Her eyes widened as she let out a sharp cry and arched, ribs straining under her smooth flesh. Her blue eyes were slits, fixed on his hot gaze. *Look what you do to me, cowboy.*

Look what you do to me, woman, he almost replied.

He held on through another of Lana's sweet cries, then tugged her close and coiled himself to roll. Enough unscheduled changes to his flight plan. He was ready for the main event. They maintained contact throughout the roll, and when they grounded out, his full weight hammered home, eliciting a cry of delight. He thought he might have acted too late, that she'd come too early, but Lana held on as he drove into her again and again. His heart leaped, wanting to give her everything at once. Hard and fast, that's what she'd asked for, right? The way her breath caught between each curt inhale and exhale told him he was getting it just right.

Hard and fast, his wolf howled in glee, as much for his own high as hers. The rumble inside him became a roar, and the roar built until he shattered inside her with a raspy groan. He rode the wave as long as he could, letting his voice underpin her high cries until both faded into whispers.

He heard the cicadas cheer their performance, the stars sing in approval. Slowly, their bodies descended from their shared climax. Heaving, panting, and sweating, they sank into each other as their mingled musk embraced the night.

He waited for the bubble to burst, for reality to set in.

Waited some more, because satisfaction this rich, this peaceful, just couldn't last. But the high refused to fade. Instead of evaporating into uncomfortable silence, it morphed into a new form: a soft, orange heat, like the glowing embers of a hearth. He pulled her closer and heard his wolf sigh inside.

Maybe it wasn't the end. Maybe it was only the beginning.

∞∞∞∞

Ty watched Lana stir from the nest she'd formed along his body to consider the stars. She was so close, face to face, that he felt like an extension of her.

"I think I might have to recalibrate my scale," she said. Her mouth curved into an angle that pointed somewhere between shy and sultry. "The guys I gave eights and nines to before seem more like fives now. Maybe fours."

He didn't savor the thought of her having been with anyone else, but the compliment—well, that part, he had to like. And he had to agree.

"Or maybe forbidden fruit tastes the best," she whispered, growing morose.

None of that, not now. He squeezed her close and let his eyes travel up the sides of the truck. "You deserve better than this."

Better than this? Lana tucked her cheek against his neck. *No way.*

He had to smile. "Yes, way. Just wait 'til I get you to a bed." What started as a chuckle ended in a whisper as it dawned on him. She'd only thought the words, not actually voiced them.

Lana's head popped up, eyebrows bunched. *Dang, can you actually hear my thoughts?*

Sometimes, he said, watching her jaw go slack. Siblings and packmates could hear each other's thoughts, but it shouldn't be possible for two near-strangers. Yet he and Lana heard each other loud and clear.

Before he could dissect that impossibility, a noise tugged at the fringe of his senses. He looked out, past the soft flesh of her breasts, past the parallel lines of her abdomen, highlighted in shades of midnight gray.

"What?"

He shushed her, listening. Headlights sliced through the dark as a laboring truck came their way from a distance. "Cody," he groaned, then jackknifed up. He offered Lana his hand and wrapped his flannel shirt around her naked frame for the second time that night.

"Is there somewhere we can go?" she asked, a millimeter from his lips.

He looked beyond her, into the hills. There was a place. His private hideaway. He'd never brought a woman there before. That rule was carved in stone.

But all it took was one look at Lana for bedrock to tremble and give way.

∞∞∞

They were dressed and bumping down the road again before Cody could draw up beside them. Lust hummed in Ty's veins as the truck rolled over the gravel road, patient in the knowledge that he'd have her again soon. Because he wasn't going to let this woman go. Not tonight. Not for many nights, not if he could help it. Families be damned. Bloodline be damned. His father, her father—what would they really do?

He wasn't about to hide her, either. That would be impossible now, anyway. His scent was all over her. So everyone would know. So what?

His eye twitched at the thought of his father's impending return. *If ever a Dixon was to step foot here...*

Lana rubbed her bare thigh with a palm and leaned back with a smile that said she was savoring a simmering memory. "You're very thorough. Covered me well and good with your scent, alpha."

Damn, that would take some getting used to. A woman reading *his* thoughts? He fought back the grin growing on his lips. The idea had its own crazy appeal.

He met her eyes, and the steady calm he found there was a salve to his troubled soul. His wolf was right. She could do it. He'd met the one woman who could temper him, stand beside him—

A snake slithered across the road and he jerked the wheel to swerve. He shook off the sense of unease it brought, determined not to let anything ruin this glorious night.

"So beautiful here," Lana murmured as mesquite and pinyons slid past, waving to her like visiting royalty. She smiled back at them as if promising to come back soon and meet each one of them. His eyes roamed over the landscape, trying to imagine it from her perspective. What did she think of the yucca, sticking up like a scarecrow? Or the ragged-barked walnut standing sentry over there? To him, the desert had always been soothing despite its rugged edges. Home.

Lana's next comment nearly gave him whiplash. "It hasn't changed a bit."

His teeth caught on his lips. It took two tries to get the words out. "What do you mean?"

"I figured it would have changed since the last time I was here, but it hasn't. So peaceful."

"You were here before? When?" His voice dropped an octave.

"It would have been... May. Twelve years ago? Thirteen?" Lana paused, checking her memory. "The year the pump house burned down. I remember everyone talking about it." She looked at him closely, some private thought playing in those eyes. "How is it that we didn't meet then?"

His mind whirled. Where had he been in May of that year? Some dim memory stirred, then clouded when Lana's eyes jumped to left side of the road. "Hmpf," she mumbled, suddenly distracted. "What do you keep up there?"

"Up where?"

She pointed up a gully.

"Just bush up there," he assured her, still groping for the memory.

"I saw something. Trash maybe?"

He snorted. "Nothing out there."

70

He felt her go tense at the blunt dismissal in his words. Crap. This was just as bad as whipping the luggage out of her hand. Why couldn't he get this right?

Lana's head swiveled as the truck rolled on, clearly reluctant to give up on whatever she'd spotted in the black streak in the landscape. Really, though, what would there be up there?

But what if? When Lana put a hand on his arm, he pulled the truck to a stop and turned to face her. Lana stubbornly held his gaze, and his wolf stirred again. *Look at her! Not even a blink!*

The blue of her eyes was unperturbed. It was only the sideways tilt of her head that said she didn't like what she'd seen up in the hills.

He put the truck in reverse and let it roll backward. If she was so sure something was amiss, he'd better check it out. "Where?"

Lana leaned over, reaching across his body to search outside his side window. For a moment, all he could sense was her pure, flowery scent. He wrapped an arm around her waist, and tugged her closer, reaching with his lips. He would have lost himself in her body again had it not been for Cody's truck pulling up behind them.

He gave himself a little shake, then broke away from Lana and turned off the engine. If only it was as easy to settle his raging pulse.

"Up there," Lana pointed.

Cody's headlights filled the cab, and Ty slipped outside. A door slammed, and his brother joined him in silent contemplation of the hills.

"What?" Cody ventured.

"Lana saw something up there," he said as she stepped to his side and exchanged a nod of greeting with his brother.

Cody must have caught the way he slid an arm around her waist, like he meant to hold on, not just for tonight but forever, because suddenly he was wildly signaling his doubts.

You know who she is, Cody started. *Are you crazy?*

Ty could imagine the rest. It was one thing to enjoy a woman for one night, but to contemplate keeping one? And

71

not just any woman, but a Dixon? He should never have told Cody about the feud.

You're playing with fire. Dad is going to skin you alive—

He shoved a hand flat against his brother's chest, letting his eyes flare until Cody wilted and raised his hands in defeat.

Lana was not a choice; she was a necessity. He knew that now. This wasn't about pleasure or a fleeting thrill. He needed her to become part of him. The fact that they could hear each other's thoughts, clear as day, was proof of that.

Lana wasn't an outsider. She belonged here, with him.

He was consumed with the need to possess her. Nothing but the mating call could do this to a wolf. But then again, he thought he'd heard the call once before. Long ago, when he'd caught that phantom scent on the wind.

The voice of doubt returned. Maybe he was kidding himself, letting one hot night carry him away. He'd go crazy trying to figure it all out in one night, though, and there was more pressing business right now. He set off up the gully, Cody and Lana following close behind. They climbed one hundred yards, scraping along the loose dirt and picking their way around wait-a-whiles. He stopped and cast his eyes around as Lana scrambled higher. Cody was right; there was nothing.

"Up here," Lana called.

He swung up in six long strides, Cody's skeptical step a tick slower behind him.

"There," she pointed.

How she'd caught the glint of broken glass from way down on the road, he couldn't tell. But a wave of silent pride swelled in him as Cody did a double take. *Man, she's good.*

Mine, he growled back.

Cody put his hands up. *All right already!*

The ground was littered with shattered beer bottles. Lana edged around the shards on nimble, bare feet and craned her head toward a spot higher up. Mumbling, she set off up the steep slope. Doubled over the way she was, the flannel shirt barely covered her glorious ass. He shot a mental bark at his brother, and Cody averted his eyes.

"Here," Lana called.

He scaled the slope, catching the scent of ashes before his eyes found a burned-out campfire. The ashy smell covered the scent of dried blood, and he studied the hollow until his eyes confirmed what his nose had already registered. There was a desiccated pile of sheep bones stuck with bits of matted wool. The place had been used as a temporary camp.

He exchanged looks with Cody. The rogue coyotes. It had to be.

Lana's nose crinkled, probably as much from the fight that had scarred her as the smell. "Three days old, maybe?"

Close. More like two. The desert worked that fast.

"What do you think?" Cody asked. "Four of them? Five?"

He only nodded vaguely. "Enough to make trouble."

Big trouble, Cody agreed.

"About as old as the dead sheep back there, right?" Lana waved toward where they'd met the Seymour ranchers, and a second stab of pride registered in him. He watched as Lana pointed around the campsite, reconstructing the scene. "So they stopped here and ate their fill. And then?" She looked from him to Cody, then back.

Exactly the question he was asking himself. Where were they now? Where would they strike next?

Lana kicked the dirt. "Fresh enough trail," she murmured, sniffing the air like she was considering going after it herself. "You got a good tracker?"

He nodded. They had a few. Kyle, for one. Zack was another, but he was still off hunting with his mate. For an instant, Ty wished he could follow the rogue trail himself. He was a good tracker—a damn good one. But as alpha, he didn't get to do that any more. He had to delegate, even when he wished he could do it all himself. Right now, he wanted nothing more than to follow the trail and rip the rogues to shreds. For trespassing on pack territory, not to mention interrupting his night with Lana.

Lana. He wanted her again. But he had duties to fulfill...

Something his sister Tina had been saying for years echoed in his mind. *Give Cody more responsibility. We lead as a*

73

family. He studied his brother in the moonlight. Had he finally matured enough to be trusted?

Lana paced, looking for more clues, bare legs poking a long way out from under the flannel shirt. Ty caught himself looking a little too long, a little too closely and gave himself an inner pinch. Now he was the one who was dazed to distraction by a female, while Cody, of all people, was on track.

So let Cody handle it.

The rogues would strike again, but not tonight. He could feel that much in the air. He could afford to take the rest of the night off.

"Cody will take care of it," he announced.

Cody went wide-eyed. *I will?*

He made his instructions quick and clear, so that even his little brother couldn't mess them up. "Get back home and double the night watch. Assemble the trackers by first light. Got it?"

"Got it, got it," Cody echoed, double timing it back to his truck.

He could feel the heat rise in his cheeks as he gave the orders. The very thought of trespassers on ranch land, even here on the periphery, pissed him off. But when Lana pressed to his side, his heat slid from anger over to desire. They weren't finished for the night. Not by a long shot.

Chapter Nine

The world was tipping sideways and Ty wasn't even trying to hang on.

He watched Cody leave in a plume of pale dust. Anticipation and the glorious sense of letting duty go, if only for one night, danced inside him as he and Lana climbed back in the truck and resumed their drive. A few minutes later, he turned off the main track, putting the truck in low gear to grind up the rough, serpentine path. Would she like his cabin in the hills? Would she feel at home there?

The thought brought a hail of laughter from his wolf. Something about the bachelor falling hard.

Whose side was the animal on, anyway? *If you want to share, play nice.*

The wolf promptly shut up.

Lana stroked his arm, sending little ripples of soothing heat through his body. He hadn't even realized he'd tensed up until her touch eased it out of him. So much that his mind slid back off track with renewed lust.

"Keep touching me and you'll find yourself in the back of the truck again." His voice was all gravel, swirling at the bottom of a mountain stream, but Lana only smiled. "That or right here," he finished, shaking his head at himself, his hands searching for a dry grip on the steering wheel.

Lana tilted her head back in silent amusement. *Is that a promise?*

Yeah, she knew right where she had him, and she liked it, too. The funny thing was, his wolf didn't protest her power over him.

He tried not to dissect the thought too much as he drove on. When they finally reached the end of the track, he brought the truck to a halt with its bumper pushing against the bushes. He sighed, thinking how long it had been since he'd been up there. There'd been too many fires to put out down at the ranch lately. The sooner he erased the rogue problem, the sooner he and Lana would have time for more nights up here. More time for each other.

The truck was still swinging gently on its chassis when she turned to face him, a question in her eyes.

"We have to walk the rest of the way," he said. "It's not very far." Still not close enough for his appetite, though.

Damn, he gulped, *she really must be reading my mind.* Because Lana's hand went to the top button of her shirt—his shirt—in a move that was anything but innocent. She slipped the button open, then the next. His lips ticked with desire as his eyes followed along. She slipped out of the passenger door and stood outside, the wide V at her neck hinting at the swell of her breast. In one smooth move, she tugged the shirt off and tossed it into the cab.

Thump, went his heart, and the heavy sensation echoed in his groin. Lana stood as naked as she'd been at the beginning of this crazy night, waiting for him. He yanked his T-shirt over his head and swung his door open.

"Beat you to the top," she called with a grin.

His jaw dropped as her finely coiled ass raced into the bush. He could already hear the pattern of her footsteps change from two to four. Ty dropped his pants in record time and shifted, following her cue.

Brush and brambles dragged along his thick fur, but all he felt was the rush of the chase. He bared his teeth in excitement. Damn, but the she-wolf could run. He thundered after her but only came within reach of her taupe rump on the last bend. He closed in, lust pulsing through his body. But Lana just flipped her tail and leaped away, teasing him again. His blood pressure rose a notch as he kicked into high gear. He was beginning to think she might actually beat him to the front step when he knocked into her from behind.

Gotcha. He grinned in triumph, even though he suspected it was the other way around. Lana had a way of turning everything upside down. Yep, there it was, a triumphant look in her flashing eyes. She'd slowed at the last minute to let him catch up. His masculine pride would have been a lot more hurt if not for the fact that he was halfway up her back. The tufts of her ears were within snapping distance of his muzzle and for a moment, he was tempted to take her the wolf way. It would be so easy, so good.

Yet he hesitated. This woman was so different than any he'd ever met. Didn't she deserve better than a hot, hard screw in the dark?

He rubbed his muzzle against the ruff of her neck. The tips of her ears were silk against the coarse stubble of his chin, and she gave a light growl of pleasure, coaxing him in with a brush of her hips.

Tempted. He was sorely tempted. But he wavered. He wanted to offer her something more than quick fuck. A lot better, and not just in terms of physical pleasure.

He stepped back and shifted, pulling himself to his full human height. The transformation was smooth and effortless, a sign that his wolf agreed. The question was, would Lana's wolf agree?

He waited with baited breath. Her long-legged wolf was as seductive as her human one was, in that same spitfire way. Absolutely perfect, from the sheen of her brown coat to the bright blue of her eyes. Was he nuts for restraining himself?

But the fact was, he wanted all of her—the woman and the wolf. The latter harbored her instincts and passions. Her human side, though, was the seat of her mind, her heart, her principles. If he wanted to win this woman over, it was that side he would have to prove himself to.

The fact that he even wanted to win her over, that he even cared, struck him with its novelty. There were a hundred reasons they ought to stay apart, yet all he wanted was for them to be together. Together for good.

For good, his wolf echoed.

He squatted and reached a cautious hand toward her wolf, palm up. There was a time to be alpha, and a time to be an equal. Ty prayed he would remember how.

Lana's eyes flashed, then softened, and she let out a slow breath. Slowly, her canine features blurred and gave way to her human shape in a rolling motion that left her seated on the ground before him. She leaned back on her elbows and considered him as her hair flowed over a shoulder, exposing her bare breasts.

"Alpha," she growled in a low voice that said her inner beast was barely leashed, "You better not be turning me down again." It was a warning, a protest. Her pose, however, was all tease. Her bent knees spread slightly apart, inviting him in.

God, he loved her pluck. He leaned into her space, pulse hammering. "She-wolf," he rumbled, "you will never doubt me again."

A ripple of laughter went through her naked body, and her breasts—the only soft flesh amidst lean muscle and taut skin—quaked with it. The movement sent an answering twitch through his cock.

"Oh, no?" she teased, leaning back farther and making space for him to kneel between her legs.

He sank an arm on either side of her body and came to within a hair's breadth of her lips. "No."

"Never?" she asked, eyes sparkling as her legs squeezed along his sides.

"Never." He managed those two syllables, then fell into a hungry kiss. It was bold, possessive, demanding, but he couldn't hold back. The wolf was close to taking over now. When Lana gave back in kind, the thin line between man and wolf merged and he eased her to the ground, locking her body beneath his and tugging her arms up over her head.

"You sure you want this?" he asked when he came up for air. Yeah, he was a little late in asking, but he had to be sure.

Her body was tight and hard, yet it wasn't fighting his weight. On the contrary, she was pushing herself closer. "Don't you dare stop, wolf," she said then devoured his mouth with hers.

He clamped both her hands in one of his and let the other sweep along her body until it found the warm swell of her breast. He lowered his chin and let his lips follow the same path until they tightened over her right nipple. Her scent, taste, feel—he chased after each in turn, his mind jumping wildly from one to the other and back again. He switched from one nipple to the other and nipped just hard enough for her to cry out, even as the arch of her back demanded more. He wondered how long he could hold out this time.

Whether it was him or her who initiated the turn, he didn't know. All he knew was that a minute later, she was on her hands and knees and he was bent over her from behind, running his hands over smooth feminine flesh that begged for instant gratification. He skimmed his palms over her shoulder blades, then followed the line of her ribs around and up, until he had her breasts cupped in two perfect handfuls. They were the only thing about Lana that might be called small or delicate—but they were perfect, just like the rest of her.

That was about as far as the man's mind got before the wolf took command of his human body. He growled right into Lana's ear—*Mine! Mate!*—pulled her hips close, and let his cock slide home.

Part of him wanted to pound his chest and roar as he sank in to her then pulled back and hammered home again. *Mine!* Another withdrawal, another powerful thrust. *Mate!*

He found a better grip on her waist, and pushed in again, sliding hot and deliciously deep. His wolf was pushing Lana hard, but she didn't give any sign of protest. On the contrary, she rammed her hips back to meet each push with a moan.

Yes, she grunted in his mind. *There'll be time for gentle later. I want this now. Exactly this.*

He pulled back until the very tip of his cock played at her entrance, torturing himself as much as her before plunging back in. She was slick and yielding and hot, and when he paused to relish the moment, her inner muscles squeezed hard, bringing him right to the edge of climax.

She released, letting him retreat, then return so she could do it again. He sank into her over and over, swimming in the glory of the sensation. Each time, she cried out her approval, her voice high and sweet in the dry desert air. "Ty!"

He kept his mouth shut, afraid of what he might say. Lana would be all right, but what if he blurted out something like *Love* or *Mate*? Was he ready for that?

Yes! his wolf sang. *Yes!*

They repeated the move again and again until they were both humming with the pleasure of it. A moment later, the steady metronome went wild, tipping from perfectly timed pleasure to sheer overpowering need. When his final thrust hit deep, he exploded inside and took Lana with him into a hot, screaming free fall he never wanted to end.

They sank to the earth and lay clasped tight, panting. Time became a blur, as if the laws of physics were trying to catch up with what they'd just done. His body blurred, too, going from warm and languid to increasingly heated, until his the wolf sprang out, finally freed for his turn. Lana shifted, too, and they hit a second wind, taking off on another wild chase that brought them in on a wide arc of the hill until they came in sight of the cabin where he caught her at last.

When they paired as wolves, every cell of his body howled with the thrill. Never, ever, had he been with a woman in both human and wolf form, let alone in the same night. As a wolf, he could unleash his animal side without fear, but it felt right that they'd let their human bodies unite first. Because this was more than a moonlit romp. It was a prelude to something bigger and better. The desert, the night, the stars—all of them leaned in and smiled with that same promise.

Then he and Lana were curled together on the ground, nuzzling their thick necks in a lazy, intimate dance. He lost himself in her, letting the line between their bodies blur. Wolves weren't big on pillow talk—thank God—but they were masters of the post-coital nuzzle.

Lana's tongue caressed his ear for long, languid minutes, melting his insides. She was incredible. And she was his. The realization should have ripped through him like a bullet, but it spread slowly, like an oil lamp gradually illuminating the truth. As if it were inevitable, and he'd known all along.

Because everything was clear to him now.

May, all those years ago. The year the pump house burned down. She'd visited the ranch back then. How, why, he didn't know. The critical thing was the date. That was the first time his father had taken him along to answer a call for help from another wolf pack. Twelve years ago.

He'd come home and caught the faint hint of a scent carried by the wind. He'd lost his heart to a phantom—the one wolf whose scent promised the kind of bond only possible with a destined mate.

Twelve years ago, Lana had visited the ranch, but she'd left before he returned.

The phantom and Lana were one and the same.

He buried his face in her neck, trying to hide the tremble inside.

Chapter Ten

Ty sucked in a long, deep breath. All those years ago, he'd fallen for Lana, even without having a face to put with the scent. These last few days, he'd done it all over again. And now he knew. It had been her all along. Her, only her.

Maybe he wasn't a faithless bastard like his father, after all.

He could have beat his head against the ground at his own thick-headedness. How could he not have recognized it sooner? Maybe because Lana's scent had been so faint back then, masked by a thousand desert flowers. And her scent would also have matured over time.

Matured. His mind grabbed at the word. That was it. Lana would have been very young back then; him, too. He had to marvel at it all. Fate had hidden them from each other until they were both ready.

Ready to stand up to the wrath of his father? He wrapped his body tighter around Lana's. Yes, even that. Just a few years ago, he stood up to his father to refuse an arranged mate. Getting his father to accept a sworn enemy into the pack would be even harder, but the reward would be forever. He'd never let Lana slip away again. Never.

His Dad would just have to suck it up. It was his life, his heart.

No wonder he couldn't get enough of her. He wasn't just quenching the thirst of a few days—more than a decade of longing was finally finding relief.

An easy, slow-motion feeling washed over him. For the first time in a long time, he felt like destiny was smiling on him. Soon, he knew, she would let him bite deep and take her as his mate—forever. Knowing Lana, she'd have her own bite ready for him, too. His heart skipped as he imagined their life together, with her filling his heart and his home, always there for him with a soothing touch and a smile that lit the fire of his passion. With her, he could truly live and not simply exist.

When Lana pulled away, he let out a whine of protest until she touched him again—with human hands now, stroking delicately around his ears, from the thick ruff of the base all the way to the razor edges. He found himself humming with pleasure as he looked up at her bare form in the moonlight. Disjointed words flitted through his mind, words like *heaven* and *beautiful* and *right*. Not that words mattered; a wolf didn't need poetry to celebrate love.

Lana bent low and puffed into his ear, then stood and waited on the top step of the cabin. The moonlight cast her bare body in a pale, mystical light. Did she realize they were destined for each other?

He should tell her immediately about the phantom, about the time he'd spent searching for her. He should explain that fate was on their side. But then again, maybe now was not the time, and God knew speeches were not his forte. No, he'd tell her everything once they were inside. Better yet, he'd wait until sunrise. A new day, a new start. A new life together. They would figure out the details soon enough.

For now, though, he would let go and slide into this glorious feast of the senses. He indulged in a long, wolf stretch, hips up and back, shoulders low. He shifted back into his human body as he stepped toward the porch, barely registering the flash of pain that accompanied the change. Still tingling, he tucked his face alongside her cheek, his chest pressed to her breast. Heaven, indeed.

"Sorry," he murmured.

"You're apologizing?" she said, waiting for the punchline.

He worked his jaw a little, summoning words. "It was supposed to be slow and...what was it?"

She cupped his face with both hands and kissed him deep. "Sensual," she murmured, illustrating with her tongue. Jesus, did she have a way with that word.

Slow. Sensual.

Hell, it was worth a try.

∞∞∞∞

Lana was sweating despite the chilly night air. She had to chuckle at herself. So much for not acting like a bitch in heat.

She sighed, inside and out, and her wolf nodded smugly. *Okay*, she admitted to the beast, *you were right*. If she hadn't pushed Ty, this might not have happened.

She and Ty belonged together. It was impossible to deny, given the way every electron in her body seemed aligned to Ty's magnetic north. She let herself glow in the thought for a moment before anxiety butted into her thoughts like a snorting bull. What if she was wrong? What if she was over-interpreting their connection? She took a deep breath of desert air, and though it was dry, it went down smooth and easy. Somehow, it didn't feel like their first night together. No, this *had* to be right.

Her pulse was racing even now. Just looking at him did that to her. She nearly let out a giggle. Like most wolves, she had a few wild, full moon nights to her credit, but never anything quite like this. To begin with, she'd always kept her two sides apart, human and wolf. But with Ty, she'd crossed over and back, seamlessly. Human, wolf, human. With him, it was one and the same. Her wolf had never demanded anything beyond physical thrills, but now she was howling crazy ballads of love and belonging—and her human side was humming the very same tune.

She steadied herself against a thick beam of the cabin and looked down across the valley. The deep porch would be as inviting in the heat of the day as it was now. The breeze was stronger up here in the hills, and the rest of the world seemed far, far away.

Ty stepped close, and she couldn't wait to have him again. On her, in her. All over. Every inch of her body yearned for his touch. "This place is beautiful," she whispered into his lips.

"You're beautiful," he growled.

She chuckled. "You're purring, wolf."

"Nmmm," he murmured, and the sound reverberated in her ear. "Wolves don't purr."

"This one does."

"Then you're the one doing it to me." He kissed her purposefully, like he was working his way down a wish list. The next kiss went deeper, promising drawn-out sex that would leave no stone unturned.

As if I have any of those left, she laughed to herself.

Is that a dare?

She didn't know what stunned her more—the easy way they could communicate or the playful twinkle in his eyes. Somehow, she'd never imagined connecting that particular adjective with Ty. Him, playful?

Dare taken, he nodded through the next kiss.

He led her into the cabin, kissed her and deposited her gently on the massive bed, then padded away. Lana heard a drawer slide, the scratch of a match. A faint glow flickered over Ty's cheeks, then licked blue across the wick of a lantern. She quivered when he blew out the match, the circle of his mouth sending a thrill straight to her core. Playful wasn't the word for him, now. Sensual was more like it. The man was true to his word.

The lantern revealed a small, simple cabin. Overhead, the open rafters hung with wispy reminders of years past. A masculine hideaway that didn't hold a female scent. Not a trace.

"My brother and I built this place," he said, circling the bed with the lantern, his cock erect.

She rolled, following him with her eyes, transfixed by the light and the sight of his body. She wanted to mark him the way he'd marked her, rubbing against him until his scent was indistinguishable from hers.

Ty set the lantern down amidst a clutch of devil's claws on the bedside table, then settled along her body, matching their lengths. His eyes met hers from behind long, dark lashes that contradicted his rougher edges. Starting slowly, he rubbed her shoulder in circles until she cooed in delight.

"For a wolf, you're pretty damn good at sensual," she sighed, combing her fingers through his hair and finding it dewy with sweat.

"You define sensual," he murmured, letting his stubble scour her breast.

She was getting sucked in way over her head. But oh, it felt good. Never mind the thing about a feud. So her mother had been with Ty's father, once upon a time. Weird, but okay, everyone had a past. That their fathers had gone from friends to sworn enemies had nothing to do with her love for Ty.

Yes, love. She loved him. She wasn't sure how it was possible, but destiny's kind of chemistry wasn't something you could analyze in a lab. It was the way it was. When the time came, she and Ty would face his father together and show him they were serious.

The question was, would the man listen? And what about the rest of the pack? Who would they side with?

The questions bumped uneasily through her mind. Maybe she was getting ahead of herself. It wasn't like Ty had declared any feelings for her, after all. From the moment she'd first kissed him, everything had started rolling out of control, faster and faster. So fast that she worried about destiny falling behind. She was a passenger on a runaway train about to jump its tracks and the conductor was nowhere in sight. All she could do was hang on to the wild ride and hope that momentum would carry them through.

Ty's lips closed around her nipple then, pushing away her anxious thoughts. Though her vision only registered shades of yellow-gray in the lantern light, she'd never felt so immersed in sensation. Ty's breath at her breast, the honeydew of his tongue. The feel of his short, silky hair between her fingers. A trace of wolf stayed with the man, together with the scent of sage, earthy and fresh. She wanted to memorize every heartbeat of this night. The tickle when he reached the top of her thigh, the heady bubble of pleasure when his fingers slipped inside.

Slow and sensual. The man was a natural.

When their bodies locked together at last, their movements were unrushed, like the long days of summer. They swayed in a gradual escalation of motion and sensation that brought them to their highest peak yet. It wasn't cliffy or steep like those that had topped their earlier rounds, but rather a smooth, round dome with views all around—a panorama of the past, the present, even a hint of a promising future. When they both came in the very same breath, the climax didn't push them blindly off the heights but sent them into a long, easy slide into a new valley. A secret Eden no one but them was allowed to enter.

A place called home, where their souls joined as one.

Afterwards, she stroked Ty's chest until the tight cords of muscle eased into slumber. It was deep in the night. The moon was in the west, a few hours away from setting. She felt so warm next to Ty, so secure. And yet this man was so much more than just raw, gritty power. He'd revealed an incredibly tender side, too, stroking her long after the act, the motion seeming to soothe him as much as it did her.

She looked back on the night, trying to make sense of her feelings. The first time, in the truck, had been all about lust. Outside the cabin—that was thrill with an undercurrent of possession. But this last round? This gloriously soft, silky sex? That went deeper.

She wondered what emotions they might cycle through if they kept this up. Admiration? Respect? Love? Or just bitter disappointment. Even regret.

She rested her chin on Ty's chest and watched him sleep, her fingers tracing the curves of his shoulder. She wanted to etch every detail of this beautiful night into her memory. Just in case.

∞∞∞∞

Ty floated through the night, plastered to Lana as if someone had brushed her with glue, then pressed her to him. Except that person was himself, architect of his own predicament. He wanted to relish this short peace, this calm before the storm, yet something nagged at him, even in sleep. He tried swatting it away. Why leave this perfect spot he'd found somewhere between her left breast and hip?

But Lana was nudging him. "Ty, someone's coming," she whispered, her muscles wound tight.

His left ear flicked at the sound of an engine. Then came a squeak of brakes, the creak of a chassis, and the thump of a door closing. He stretched slowly, then sat up with a jolt, sniffing. Had he really slept so soundly that he'd missed someone's approach?

He sniffed again and cursed. "Cody." Why the fool was coming to the cabin to disturb the most glorious sleep of his life was a mystery to his hazy mind. But two things were very, very clear in the dusty pink of the pre-dawn sky. He was keeping this woman forever, and he was going to kill his brother.

Cody came crashing up the path to warn them of his approach, then cleared his throat on the stoop for two long minutes before finally calling through the open door. "Uh, Ty?"

He let his growl fill the still cabin. "It better be damn important."

"It is, it is." Cody's voice barely trusted itself past the door frame. "Sorry!"

You better be. He rolled away from Lana and pushed himself up, feeling heavy and spent. Pack business, always pack business. He covered the distance to the door slowly and leaned a weary shoulder against the frame.

Cody's hands tunneled into his pockets like maybe if he bored deep enough, the rest of him could hide in there, too. Yeah, he knew just how pissed Ty was. Good.

Still, the reason for his brother's visit couldn't be good. He raised a hand to scratch at his ear, but stopped halfway as Lana's soft step resonated through the floorboards. He couldn't suppress a twinge when her naked body tucked behind his, soothing and inquiring at the same time. Her fingers intertwined with his, giving them something much better to do that maul his own skin. He felt a new rush, one that had nothing to do with taking her back to bed. She was offering him all her inner strength and encouragement. He imagined facing his duties with that kind of support. Jesus, how different his life would be.

It wasn't that he minded what he had to do. Hell, he lived for it, but he longed for more. Love. Companionship. Comfort. The words came rolling through his mind, all by themselves. Lana could give him all that, and more. She would shore him up, not weaken him. She could stand up to his power without fading away. With her, he could carve out a small space for his soul within the demands of the alpha role. Hope straightened his shoulders, even as they struggled under the implied threat weighing down the air.

"Good morning, Cody," Lana murmured, peeking out from beside his shoulder. He curled a possessive arm backwards, just in case his little brother didn't get the message.

Cody shifted back. Way back. Message received. "Morning." He tipped his hat with that boyish smile that managed to melt just about every female.

Lana showed no reaction. She just nodded, sending a wave of satisfaction through him. A feeling that faded with Cody's next words.

"We got trouble, Ty."

Chapter Eleven

Lana parked Cody's truck in its usual spot, just inside the ranch gate. Back at the cabin, Ty had kissed her goodbye before going off with his brother to examine the scene of what appeared to be another rogue incursion. It was a hurried kiss full of unspoken promises—all but the one she'd managed to extract before he left.

"Promise me you won't run off to fight without me." Her voice wavered as she tugged him close.

Ty's eyes were darker than ever as he pulled back to study her closely. "Lana," he started, reluctance weighing on his lips.

She tightened her grip on the front of his shirt. "Promise!" She let her expression say the rest. That she was damn good in a fight. That she'd fought off rogues before. That she'd do anything for him, and anything to gain the respect she deserved in his pack.

His eyes searched hers a moment longer before he nodded, then pulled her into a last embrace. One that spun her dizzy inside, even though his lips were the only things moving.

When Ty broke away and drove off with Cody, she could practically see the burden of responsibility clamp down on his shoulders. She kicked at the dirt, then drove back home to the ranch. Alone.

Wait. Home?

She decided not to examine that one just now. She had enough on her mind. Enough to give the steering wheel a frustrated punch after parking the car. Damn it, she could help! Back in the Berkshires, she fought on the front line alongside her brothers. None of this women-stay-back-at-the-ranch nonsense. She and Ty could fight together through any obstacle the outside world could conjure: fathers, feuds, rogues. They'd conquer it all together, or die trying.

But this wasn't her pack, no matter how much her heart leaped at the notion. One night with the alpha—no matter how delicious—hardly qualified her for special privileges. She knew she'd have to tread very carefully. She and Ty would have to face his father soon, and it wouldn't be pretty. The thought had her hugging Ty's shirt more closely around her as she stamped over to the guest house. She took a quick shower, deep in thought, then headed over for breakfast with her grandmother and Jean.

"Did you have a nice night, dear?" Jean leaned in for a kiss. "Oh. Oh my."

Her grandmother looked over with raised eyebrows, and Lana shrank back. The women were old, but their noses missed nothing.

"Oh, you did have a good night," Nan observed, and the older women giggled as her face went hot. She wished for the thousandth time that her kind weren't able to scent every single emotion, every change in physical state.

Jean waved Lana to the breakfast table and winked at Ruth. "What do you think is redder, her face or the jam?"

"Oh, definitely her face."

She buried her head in her hands. "Please don't tease me," she mumbled, suddenly very, very tired as the older women broke into stories of their own conquests and mornings-after.

"That lovely Baker boy, you remember him, Jean?" Nan was going on. "What big hands he had."

Her hands flew to her burning ears. *Too much information.* Then something clicked and she shifted from embarrassment to outrage. "You knew about Mom and Ty's father!" Her grandmother and Jean exchanged knowing glances. "Why did you bring me out here? Why?"

Nan smiled kindly. "Because I knew there was something special for you out here, dear."

Jean murmured in agreement. "Someone."

Her heart stumbled over the next few beats.

Nan went on. "The sky, the space. The spirit of this place. The first time we came—you remember?"

How could she forget?

"I knew you belonged here. I wanted you to see it again, to feel it, to taste it." She flashed a naughty smile. "No innuendo intended."

"Nan!" she protested. The heat in her cheeks told her they'd blazed right past red and deep into purple.

"You never seemed quite settled in the east," her grandmother continued. Lana found herself looking at her lap; it was true. "I wanted to give you a second chance."

She jerked her chin up. "At what?"

Her grandmother smiled coyly. "To finish what you started, last time we came."

She had a thousand questions, but Jean butted in with a sly look. "Breakfast first."

∞∞∞∞

Lana stared out the picture windows of Jean's house and took in the endless view. It was so much grander than the tight, green views of home. Stark and dangerous, yet exhilarating, too. Much as she loved the Berkshires, the desert tugged at something in her soul.

"How could Mom ever leave this place?"

Her grandmother gave her a sad smile. "Because your father offered her something Tyrone Hawthorne never could. Love."

She pulled in a long, careful breath, as if speaking the word aloud might jinx everything.

That was all she got out of the two older women. They were stubbornly elusive, hinting rather than telling, insisting she had to find her own path. No matter how hard Lana pressed, they refused to explain themselves. Finally, she stamped away, drained. *Fine*, she huffed. She'd drop into bed for an hour or two, then try to make sense of it all.

When she awoke in the guest house and stretched, she checked the clock. Twice. That hour or two had stretched

93

to six. Apparently, a long night of spectacularly fulfilling sex had taken its toll on her. Was Ty feeling it, too?

She wandered outside, hoping for a glimpse of him and immediately sensed that something was going on. Something big. The serenity of the ranch had been replaced by a leaden silence. The few pack members who were out and about wore dark looks and sniffed the air anxiously. Even old Jean seemed unsettled when Lana stopped by, rattling her teacup and jumping at every sound. Where were the rogues? What had the scouts discovered?

When she finally did catch a glimpse of Ty in the center of a huddle of men by the ranch gate, he looked deadly and resolute. When he glanced up, his gaze traveled through the air like a shock wave. She would have given anything to read his mind now, but the armor was locked in place and buckled tight.

When Ty immediately turned his attention to the business at hand without even acknowledging her, her heart sank. Last night, everything had seemed so clear. Now, in the light of day, she wasn't so sure. There was no signal from him, not even a blip, and her mother's warnings echoed in her mind. She could never establish equal footing with an alpha. She'd be relegated to the role of cook, maid, and sometime bedmate, expected to be at her powerful mate's beck and call.

Maybe she needed to set emotion aside and think this through. Her pride, her independence, and her career were all at stake. Was she really prepared to risk everything for this man?

Yes! her wolf screamed.

The thing was, the beast was prone to seeing things in black and white. Real life was layered with nuances, and she couldn't just will them away. All Lana could do was return to the shaded porch of the guest house and sit there simmering in uncertainty.

Things only got worse when an uninvited guest appeared. Audrey, wearing a broad smile that could only mean trouble.

"Lana, I just—" Audrey started, sashaying forward with all the warmth of a rattlesnake. Then she pulled up short, sniffing.

Here it comes, she groaned. *More teasing.*

Audrey pursed her ruby-red lips and smiled. Or was that a scowl? "Welcome to the sorority, honey."

She blinked.

"So, how was it?" Audrey urged. Her words fell with the sticky drip of fresh blood.

Sorority? Her mind whirred. A group of women who had...what? Audrey leaned forward, eager to hear every luscious detail of her seismic night.

A sorority of women who'd slept with Ty? Her gut heaved as Audrey's thick lips curved into a smug smile.

Audrey had slept with Ty? Her stomach twisted into a knot.

Audrey chuckled in staccato, cutting thrusts. "Oh, it must have been good, I can tell. But of course, with Ty, it's always good."

Always? She nearly choked.

Audrey's dreamy eyes went up as if she were reveling in her own carnal memories. "He's screwed all the girls here, honey."

Her jaw swung open. "Everyone?" Did he take them all to the cabin, too? Shower them with that incomparable blend of tenderness and blazing desire? But that could hardly be called screwing. She studied Audrey. Was she just trying to rile up the new girl in town?

The blond's eyes sparkled with mischief. "He gets a piece of just about every woman who passes through here. And who would say no?"

The punch landed square in the gut, just as intended. She hadn't said anything but *yes, yes, yes.*

But what about the promise in his eyes? Had she misjudged him so badly? Lana wavered, her stomach churning. She knew it was only Audrey's word versus her wolf's love-struck heart and frankly, neither was to be trusted. God, nothing would hurt more than finding out she was just another easy fuck for Ty. The flavor of the month. The flavor of the week, for all she knew.

Her heart sank. Here she'd been, thinking Ty was the One. But maybe history was repeating itself. After all, her mother had left Arizona to escape Ty's father, a man incapable of love.

Like father, like son?

"I'll let you down easy, honey." Audrey's triumphant tone suggested just the opposite. She forced herself to meet the woman's eyes, determined to deny her the pleasure. "He's taken."

Taken? Was this another of Audrey's games?

"He's taken, well and good. Just...waiting."

"Waiting for who?" She scraped the words through the sandpaper of her throat.

Audrey's face took on a vengeful sheen as a long fingernail slashed the horizon. "Some woman he met years ago," she spat. "That's what he told Lucy after they slept together and she ran to him crying every day for a month." Every dagger that pierced Lana's heart was a bull's eye for Audrey. "He said he lost his heart to someone a long time ago. He can never love anyone but her. The bitch." Audrey sniffed, nose held high.

"Who?" She'd been so sure that their night had been the first of a lifetime. Maybe she'd been waiting so long, she couldn't recognize the difference between love and lust. She pictured Ty again. The certainty, the devotion she'd seen in his eyes. How could there be another woman in his life?

Audrey shrugged, "Who? That's the million dollar question. We think it's some tramp from over in Utah. He came back from a trip there totally smitten. Never seen a man so wrung out," she cackled in glee before letting poison seep back into her features. "Why he doesn't just take the woman and put us all out of our misery is a mystery." Audrey heaved a tragic sigh, stretched, and stood in a pose that suggested she might dust her hands off and conclude with something like *My work here is done.*

"You'll get over him," Audrey called out instead, swinging her full hips down the walkway. "We all do."

Reason and emotion went to war in her mind, and her wolf reared up inside, indignant. *Ty is ours! Ours alone! Are you going to believe this tramp over the look in our mate's eyes?*

She swallowed back the bile in her throat and shook her head. Ty was a man of honor who'd left her with a promise. If he'd ever been the player Audrey made him out to be, that was a thing of the past. The connection she had with Ty was all about the future. Still, there was no taking the sting out of Audrey's words.

She tensed as Audrey turned around for a last dig. "Maybe he'll think of you while he fights," the blonde offered in half-hearted consolation.

She froze. "What do you mean?"

Audrey shrugged in disinterest. "He's gone off to find the rogues. Finish them off."

As if it were as easy as that. Lana doubted that Audrey had experience fighting anything worse than a bad hair day. A band of rogues was a deadly threat that would require the full strength of the pack.

But wait, had Ty really left to fight without her? She pushed herself up from her chair, every muscle wound tight. He'd promised! "Where? Where did he go?"

Audrey waved a lazy hand toward the north, unconcerned. "Somewhere in the hills." From the looks of it, she would be perfectly happy to wait by the pool while the men did the fighting. Or worse, pack a picnic basket and watch from a safe distance, like one of those misguided southern belles who'd gone out to spectate at Civil War battles.

A rush of heat pumped through her body. Like hell she'd be one of those women! Like hell she'd let Ty fight without her. In the space of her next two breaths, Lana pushed past Audrey, unleashed her inner wolf, and ran for the hills. For her mate, for the enemy, for whatever grain of truth she might find.

Chapter Twelve

It was more than a point of pride. It was a point of honor. Lana was the one who found the rogue camp. She wanted to finish this as much as anyone else. She had a right, damn it!

The scar on her arm flared as she ran, fast and furious in her wolf form. That rogue fight, years ago, had claimed two of her packmates' lives. Rogues fought dirty, with the recklessness of those with nothing to lose. And while shifters were tough, they were still mortal. Lana had learned that lesson all too well. She didn't relish a battle, but she wouldn't shy away, either.

But that was only half the issue. How could Ty have gone off without her? He'd promised not to! She shook her head as she ran. If Ty had lied to her about that, he could very well be lying about other things. Maybe the whole night had been a lie.

His scent dogged her, driving her crazy with lust, love, and the first fissures of renewed heartbreak. Even as she left the valley for higher ground, his scent persisted. She paused just long enough to scratch her ear with her hind leg, annoyed. If he proved to be a deceiver, how long would it take to scrub every last trace of him away?

She'd go back East and his scent would still be there, teasing her with what could have been. Sorority. Flavor of the month. What if she was nothing to him?

Her footfalls only seemed to pound the misery further into her soul, yet Lana hammered onward, resolute. She'd show Ty how a Dixon could fight. She'd earn his respect, even if it meant losing his affection—if that hadn't all been a show.

He will be true to us! her wolf insisted.

Then let him prove it, her human side retorted.

She leaped over a rabbit hole, then forced herself to mute the competing voices. A fight called for a clear head and clear tactics. So what the hell was she doing, running off without thinking things through?

She slowed to a trot and sniffed the air, collecting her thoughts. First things first. She'd track down Ty, deal with the rogues, then deal with the rest.

A good plan, but the dry air revealed no trace of either the alpha or the rogues. Like an amateur, she was chasing shadows. She should have followed Ty's trail from the ranch instead of setting off on the basis of Audrey's vague indication.

Audrey. What if she'd been lying all along?

She stopped altogether and turned in a slow circle, testing the air for any hint of the truth. But there was nothing, only a burning emptiness. The desert hid its secrets well.

Water, she decided. She'd find some water, then start her search anew.

She sniffed her way to a relic of a creek and followed it upstream, suddenly parched. She scratched at the dry creek bed, but found nothing. Farther up, maybe? She trotted uphill, then shifted to human form when she reached a thin trickle of water. She knelt and scooped a restless handful, entirely focused on the cool liquid.

Five yards to her right, the bushes rustled, and her head whipped around. From the left came the sharp click of a snapping twig. There was a chuckle, and two men emerged from the undergrowth, one on each side.

Her eyes went to the man on the right first. He was wiry, rugged, and wicked, like the Marlboro man gone wrong. He smiled coolly at Lana in the slanting afternoon sun, letting his gaze scrape against every inch of her exposed skin.

She all but rolled her eyes. He had to be one of those mountain hermits who'd been out in the bush too long, smoking too much of who knows what. She could smell it on him. Unconcerned, she stretched to her full height and swung her head to the man on the left. He had the same calculating eyes, the same horny bulge in his natty jeans. His face and hair had a pale cast to them: not quite that of an albino, but close.

She swallowed her surprise. So what if she was naked and alone? In two steps, she'd be in the cover of the bushes. A couple more and she'd shift and race away. These pathetic humans could never match her speed. Still, it had been stupid of her to let down her guard.

Her ears twitched, picking up the sound of third man, blocking the way behind. She could sense his presence.

"Look at what we got here, boys." The pale one's lips curled into a grimace of a smile, tongue poised suggestively on his lower lip. "A visitor, at last."

The man on the right took a step nearer, breaking into a nasty grin. "We haven't had a visitor in quite some time."

Visitor? They were the trespassers here! Lana squinted against the sun and registered their strange, scratched faces and too-bright eyes for the first time. She sniffed again and felt the scar on her arm flare up. The smell of their unwashed bodies masked another scent, one she picked up too late. It was the smell of fall, of leaves left too long. Rotten, forgotten.

Rogues. The men were the coyote rogues everyone was after. She'd found them. But where was Ty?

There were three of them. No, four; there was another crouching just out of sight behind the trees. The hair on her spine prickled as her wolf pushed toward the surface.

"Don't worry," said the pale one, "we know how to show a lady a good time." Though he flashed a warm smile as he spoke, his voice carried the breath of an Arctic wind.

She gulped away the bile rising in her throat. She had to think fast. Standing naked in front of these desperadoes was only egging them on. She had to shift—now. As a wolf, she'd be better equipped to fight or flee. A male coyote would be close to her wolf size; she could take on one. Two would be tricky, but she could do it if need be.

But three? Four?

Those odds, she wouldn't bet on. Better to run and get out before the noose tightened.

"Hey, Yas, I call first go," Marlboro man chuckled to the pale one—the leader.

Yas? She'd heard that name before. The native son gone wrong. Badly wrong.

"Save a little of her for me, boys," Yas snickered, and they closed in.

She was a second ahead with her transformation, and her canines ripped out the throat of the nearest one before he had a chance to react. Warm blood flooded her mouth as she leaped into the bush, spitting out the bitter rogue taste. Her paws clawed for purchase in the dirt as the bush behind her came alive with the coyotes' excited barks. They, too, had shifted and taken up the chase.

She fled, her mind calculating as her legs raced on. She could probably outrun these coyotes, but reinforcements would feel awfully reassuring. *Ty!* she screamed, pouring everything into the inner cry. If they truly were destined mates, he would hear her.

Jesus, what a test. She listened for some answer, some sign. But there was nothing, only the drum of her feet on the hard ground and the excited yips of her pursuers. She was on her own.

One of the coyotes was nearly upon her, and another was panting up a storm not far behind. Lana put on a burst of speed but couldn't quite find her pace, not like she could in the woods of the east. This was a slalom course of cacti and bush with no discernible pattern. She dodged right, darted left, and sprinted ahead, but not quick enough.

A tawny coyote cut in front of her from upslope. A fifth one? She cursed and jumped away, having no choice but to cut left, up a winding gully. She sprang over a jumble of boulders that marked a dry stream bed, then sprinted onward as the walls of the valley grew higher on both sides. Yes, that was it—she was breaking away. She hammered around a corner and up to—

A dead end.

She skidded to a halt, nose pointing up at impossibly steep walls. No way out there, not for a wolf, not for human. Not even for a mountain goat. She wheeled, only to find two coyotes blocking the way with a third joining them. It was through them or up the cliff.

She turned tail and leaped for a high outcrop, clawing for a grip. She nearly had it, front paws scratching on rock, hindquarters scrambling, showering her pursuers in dirt. Every muscle in her body strained as she urged herself on. *Almost there—*

Fire rocketed through her back leg and a leaden weight dragged her back. She clawed desperately at air until she landed with a slam, her shoulder smashing against a rock. When she scrambled to all fours to face them, she counted five coyotes. Or were there six? She gasped in spite of herself, then spotted more movement behind her attackers.

Yas, still in human form, came sauntering up to them, his face alight with evil thrill.

Seven. Seven to one. It would be a fight to the death. Her death. The fact that she would take two or three more of them with her was little consolation.

If she'd still been in human form, she might have wailed out loud. *Ty!* What she wouldn't give to have him at her side now. But that was not to be. She was alone, now more than ever.

The coyotes circled, keeping their muzzles down and their throats covered. They were evil, not stupid. Lana did a quick calculation. She was at least as tall as them, but lighter. If they pinned her down, it would all be over. She had to stay on her feet. Her only chance was to find their weak link and somehow rip her way through.

A coyote with a long scar across one eye lunged from the right. She sidestepped with a roar that echoed off the gully walls, then swiped at his flank. She felt the gratifying tear of flesh as the coyote screamed, his pelt torn and bleeding. Two more were on her right away, but she scattered them with a ferocious slash. They beat a hasty retreat as Yas cackled something derisive.

She fought to control her breathing, concentrating on keeping her back to the rocks. Somehow, she had to break them down, one at a time.

Her head went into a spin as three of the brutes charged simultaneously. She whirled, dodging one, batting the other, trying to keep an eye on the third. Somewhere in the melee, she felt claws rip into her rump, and an instant later, sharp canines punctured her outstretched paw. She lurched off balance and they immediately pounced. Growls pounded through her head as she clawed at the ground, kicking desperately. She had to get up! She had to break loose! She had to—

She froze the instant jaws clamped over her neck, coyote canines digging to within a hair's breadth of her jugular. It was the death hold. One squeeze and her life would gush out in a crimson deluge. She hung limp in the coyote's jaws, twisted and powerless. The sour panting of her captor ruffled her fur, smelling of foul game and rotting flesh. The snarls resounding in her ears changed in pitch as the others moved in to join him. When one of them sniffed her rear, she let out a mighty kick but froze when the jaws around her neck pinched tighter. The message was clear. One move and she was dead.

The coyotes began to jostle for position, howling in glee. She closed her eyes to avoid witnessing her own rape. She'd never, ever pictured it ending like this. A fighting death would be acceptable. But this?

The coyote holding her shuffled around to make room for another who pushed at her hips. His weight was already on her, setting her torn flesh aflame. She shifted away, but two more sets of jaws bit into her, deep and hard. Three of them were holding her now, with a fourth trying to mount her. She could feel his hips thrust blindly, seeking her entrance. Another second and he'd penetrate. The same part of her body that had yawned wide to welcome Ty was now clamped hard in gritty determination, but it was only a matter of time before the coyote managed to force his way in.

She hauled her lips back in a silent snarl. She didn't want to imagine the pain, or worse, the degradation. No; she'd tear herself free first, even if it meant death. Better to bleed dry rather than grant them their sick pleasure. *On three,* her will declared.

One.

An image of Ty flashed through her mind, his hands giving hers a gentle squeeze before he eased himself down to her body. A tender moment so unlike the horror playing out in real time.

Two.

Her mind whirled through a mental slide show, and stopped at the image of Ty stepping around the bed with the lantern in his hands. That was the one she would die with, she decided, and quickly, before the beast at her rump forced his way in.

Thr—

The gully exploded with a thunderous roar and a shower of scattered rocks as half the slope gave way in a landslide. The hold on her neck went slack, and she scrambled away, grabbing at her chance to slip free within the chaos. She'd escaped the worst, and just in time. But what was going on? There seemed to be an entire army of gritty roars smothering the confused cries of the coyotes. Under it all, she heard the desperate beat of her heart drumming in her ears.

Without thinking, she lunged at a tawny form in front of her. The coyote screamed, struggled in her jaws, then went silent when she gave a neck-breaking shake. She was just releasing the limp body when a massive shape flew into her view. Lana sagged in despair, trying to blink her vision clear. No way could she take on that one. It was as big as a wolf—

It was a wolf. So huge and intense that the walls of the gully seemed to back away from him. His fur was the deepest, darkest brown. Like a creature that had sprung from the very womb of Mother Earth, possessed with a fury so great, his coat shook with it.

Ty, like she'd never seen him before.

I will rip you to pieces, Ty's roar promised the cowering coyotes. *And then I will rip you again.*

She wobbled as he stationed himself in front of her, his eyes aglow. She knew those eyes, that power, even though she'd never witnessed their intensity at this extreme.

Mine! Ty roared, and the line of coyotes trembled. She did, too. She'd never seen fury like this. And she'd never felt anything like the huge lump that formed in her throat when she realized she'd been wrong to doubt him.

The coyotes' eyes darted around as they looked for a way out. Another roar answered Ty's—a second wolf, cutting off the coyotes' retreat. The timbre of that voice could only be Cody's. She pulled her lips up in satisfaction. The rogues were the ones trapped now, with three wolves to five coyotes. Those odds, she could bet on.

Ty's eyes caught hers, warming her inner reserves. Her shoulders straightened despite the pain wracking her body.

A voice rang out, the lone human among snarling canines. "We didn't know she was yours!" cried Yas. Hidden in his words was a plea for his life.

Through the sludge of her pain, she licked her cracked lips. How quickly the tables turned.

"You should have marked her!" Yas cried, voice unsteady.

Ty's growl vibrated through the bedrock. He advanced on the rogue one deliberate step at a time, tail twitching murderously. Yas backed away, eyes low in a sign of submission. She forced herself forward even as a volley of fireworks shot through her back leg. She would fight beside Ty, not cower behind him. She would fight off her enemies and the enemies of her pack.

My pack. How right it sounded. Because Ty's roar told her all she needed to hear. He loved her with all his might, and that might was the most impressive thing she'd ever witnessed. Ty was rage personified, wholly bent on revenge. Even more so the next instant, when a coyote sprang forward in mindless desperation, setting off the fight.

The narrow space amplified the clash to a veritable battle. Her ears rang with anguished screams, grunts, and scuttling claws. She shut away her pain and snapped at a coyote trying to edge past Ty, who was tossing aside another rogue with his blood-stained jaws. Lana let loose a snarl, or tried to; the sound wasn't coming out properly. Her vision wasn't quite right, either, bouncing from single to double images dappled with spots.

By the time she finished off the scarred coyote, she was swaying and dangerously close to collapse. She blinked, watching Ty take on Yas, who had shifted into a snow-white coyote. On a wolf, that coat would have been beautiful, but on Yas, it seemed all wrong. She just hoped she remained conscious long enough to see his white fur run red.

A shadow flickered, pulling her wobbly attention around to the left. She was fading fast, bleeding from a dozen wounds, but another coyote was launching himself at Ty.

She tried to warn him but only a hoarse peep came out. The coyote was in the air, aiming for Ty's back. He was no match for the alpha but if Ty didn't see him coming, the rogue might just get a lucky strike. She pulled out a last scrap of energy and threw herself forward. Her vision became a blurry patchwork. There was Ty's dark brown coat, and a white, terrified Yas. The tawny fur of her target flashed in the foreground. Cody's voice boomed in warning, far, far away.

When her jaws closed on coarse fur, she hurled her weight to the right, dragging the coyote down. The tackle unleashed a flood of pain that threw a blindfold over her eyes. More howls and thumps followed, then her flank was on the cool earth and the gully went quiet, at least to her ears.

She lay where she'd struck the ground, counting the last, hesitant beats of her heart. Her ruff was warm and clumpy. Her rump throbbed as she lay still, feeling her life ooze away.

She sensed a warm touch, a familiar breath, and anxious snuffling. It was Ty, licking her wounds and whimpering in her ear. *Tell me you're all right*, he begged. *Tell me you're all right, my mate.*

The words came to her as if down the length of a long tunnel, and somewhere in the fog of her mind a single patch cleared.

Mate. He'd called her his mate.

For all that her body was throbbing with pain, she let her lips curl into a satisfied smile. At last, Ty knew it, too. She mustered her last scrap of energy and did her best to deliver a faint echo of his words. *Mate. My mate.*

Ty buried his face in her neck, and his scent covered her like a warm blanket. Her mate knew her. Loved her. Wanted her. He'd picked her scent out from all the others competing for his attention. What else could she wish for?

Her joy faded as the irony bit deep. Ty had recognized love just as death was elbowing its way in. She'd run out of time. They'd run out of time.

She fought back despair, clinging instead to a slender thread of hope. At least he was with her, holding her close. She let herself sink into blackness on Ty's soothing voice. The voice of her true love was the last thing she registered before slipping away into darkness.

Chapter Thirteen

Lana was expecting a tunnel of light or a pit of darkness to call her toward death. But it wasn't like that. It was like the deepest, soundest sleep, broken only by the occasional whisper.

Mate. My mate. Stay with me.

Was she dreaming? She faded in and out as time slowed, then fast-forwarded, and slowed again.

Stay with me.

It didn't feel like sleep, but it must have been, because her senses were registering a very soft, very quiet place she didn't recognize. It was warm and cozy, like a winter den she wouldn't have to emerge from for months. Her ears picked up the whir of a hummingbird, the quiet tap of a branch on the wall. Wherever it was, she never wanted to leave.

Her body throbbed, though her wounds no longer gaped wide. Yes, the soreness was proof. She was definitely alive. A soft, safe something stirred nearby, then quieted again. Lana's chest rose and fell obediently in time with a metronome ticking behind her. Maybe that's what had kept her alive after everything went dim. She finally decided to peek at her surroundings, but even then, only one eyelid fluttered open. The other followed after an uncertain pause.

They registered ocher bedding with a navy stripe and ocher walls. Sliding to the floor, her eyes slowly focused on a diamond-pattern rug in cornflower blue. Overhead, bold strips of sky were framed by timber beams. Arizona was pouring into the room through long glass panels, coaxing her senses to life.

A gentle touch registered through her sluggish nerves, rubbing soft circles into her shoulder, and she knew it could only be Ty.

She choked on his name but couldn't hold back the tears.

He folded himself carefully around her and whispered. "Lana." He paused a moment as if weighing some decision, then pressed his lips to her ear and whispered again. "Lana. My love."

The words embraced her as warmly as his body did. He said it again, holding her close, and a flurry of images passed from his mind to hers, showing the two of them together, enjoying a lifetime of love. Everything she'd ever wanted was in those images. More, in fact, than she'd ever dared wish for. She was in his arms, in his home. When her tears of fear and anger ran dry, she shed tears of joy.

Until a worry passed through her mind like a cloud in front of the sun. "What about your father?" she croaked.

"My father will accept my mate," Ty growled. The conviction in his words nearly rocked her back, and she knew he'd face his father with the same unshakable finality. She settled back against his frame, ready to close her eyes once more.

When his voice came again, it carried an uncharacteristic waver. "Why did you run off alone? Why didn't you wait for me?"

She wanted to push her face into the pillow and fade out again. How could she explain? She'd doubted his promise, doubted everything about him. About the two of them.

Well, she would never doubt again. Nothing but death would part them now, and that, she hoped, would be a long way off.

She wanted to shake the question away, but Ty shifted around to face her, insistent.

"Audrey said..." she started, then trailed off at Ty's glower. Why had she listened to her own doubts? "Audrey said you went to fight without me," she said. "So I ran to find you..." She trailed off, cursing her own stupidity.

An awkward heartbeat ticked by, then another.

"What else did Audrey say?" Ty's baritone was laced with granite.

"Doesn't matter what Audrey said," she mumbled, feeling like an utter fool. If all Ty wanted was a woman to keep at his beck and call, he could have long since had one.

"Lana, it's a small pack here. So yes, I've been with a lot of the females," he said, as if he'd read her mind. And maybe he had. One coarse thumb rubbed her cheek softly. "As a wolf. I haven't taken a human lover since I first caught your scent."

Her breath caught in her throat as his words washed over her. She went all warm, as if he was rubbing her with a balm. Ty hadn't touched a woman in over a decade. He'd been waiting all those years—for her.

"I want you. Only you."

A veil lifted from her eyes, as she realized what parallel lives they'd lived since that time when they hadn't quite met. She hadn't taken a human lover since then, either. As a wolf, well, that was different. The human world had its rules of propriety but for wolves, instincts were commands. Unmated wolves responded to nature's calls without much discrimination. It didn't mean much. But the fact that he'd waited all these years for her?

That meant everything.

Ty loved her. He cared. He was hers. All the risks she was taking in committing to this alpha, he was taking, too. His duty, his family, the fact that she was a Dixon—Ty was putting just as much on the line. But together, they'd stand strong. She looked into Ty's eyes, so deep she could make out the outline of a shared future, centuries worth.

She turned and whispered into his shoulder. "I love you."

A ripple went through his body, a release. He'd been waiting for the words, too. The last bits of tension in her shoulders loosened their hold and tripped away like tumbleweeds seeking another place to roost.

She yearned to open her body to him there and then. They'd done lust, possession, and need. The next time would be a combination of them all, and more. They would mate and seal a common destiny. But something in her hesitated.

"We can wait, my love," Ty murmured, stroking her shoulder. "You need to heal."

She went limp with relief the moment he spoke the truth. Her physical wounds were mending quickly, but her brush with

111

the coyotes left other scars that would take longer to heal. She didn't need sex right now; she needed comfort. And Ty was there for her.

She leaned back, losing herself in his arms and the downy pillow. Fluffy clouds trooped across the sky, and her eyes fluttered to a close. She let her other senses explore the house from the comfort of her little den under his arm. The warm, earth-toned bedroom felt like an extension of the bed. Beyond it, she sensed other rooms she would get to know soon. Her nose registered a fireplace. The comforting scent of burned embers was an homage to the past; the neatly stacked kindling beside it held the promise of the future—their future, ready to burn bright. There were kitchen smells, too, dominated by spicy sauces. She could picture the chili peppers, strung hot red on a line. It was cool and clean in that kitchen, bright and airy. She could feel it.

Her new home. Yes, she could get used to it here.

Ty snuggled close and whispered. "My love."

She could get used to that, too.

Beyond the living room and kitchen there was more. Space enough for a couple of cubs, when the time came.

Three, at least. It was Ty, speaking in her mind.

"Hey!" She rolled over, ready to chastise him. The man radiated satisfaction that only wavered when she winced, still sore from her wounds. "Can you hear everything I'm thinking?"

"Just some things."

She thought it over. Three cubs?

If that's okay with you, he hastened to add.

She laughed. Maybe this alpha wasn't such a tough guy, after all.

"So, what am I thinking now?" Lana lost herself in his eyes and imagined just where she'd like him to touch her next, and how. She wasn't ready for sex, but the perfect cuddle, that would be just right.

His eyes went liquid with recognition as he rearranged her in the curve of his body, wrapping around her like armor. His lips massaged her right ear with light kisses.

"I didn't say anything about kisses," she said in a happy hum.

"Those are extra. You don't like?" The moment Ty paused, she missed it. Desperately.

"I like, I like!" she said, spurring him back into action.

Slowly, gradually, she let herself relax and take it all in. Ty, strong yet tender. The house, cozy and serene. Beyond them lay the humming beauty of the desert and the endless Arizona sky. She felt her new life envelope her like a comforter, ushering in the warmth of sleep.

I like.

Ty must have agreed, because her back started to rumble from his deep inner purr.

Wolves don't purr, he murmured.

This one does. She smiled, drifting happily to sleep.

Epilogue

One week later...

"There's one more thing we have to do tonight," Ty whispered, lowering his glistening body to hers. "Are you up for it?"

A drop of sweat fell to Lana's chest and mingled with the scent of their lovemaking. She watched him rub it into her flesh with one delightfully coarse thumb, sending a shot of warmth to the embers still glowing inside. She was still coming down from her high, the mark on her neck tingling from his mating bite.

Her half-lidded eyes slid past his body, to the windows, up into the night-cloaked hills. She couldn't muster much enthusiasm for leaving the paradise of bed until she realized what he meant. A serenade of the moon. Was she up for that?

"If we take it slow." Funny how the man made her feel capable of anything. Loving. Living. Singing.

"As slow as you want," he promised.

She snorted. "As slow as you went just now?"

His face clouded over. "I didn't hurt you, did I?"

Her chuckle gave away the tease. "It was amazing." She touched the matching bite mark she'd left on his neck. It was already healing, just like her own. After a week of waiting for exactly the right moment, they'd finally marked each other as mates for life. A faint scar would remain as symbol of their eternal link. Her hand slid to Ty's chest and rested there, feeling his heart rate settle as his fingers wrapped around hers. Going for the blood bond while making love had produced a shattering climax for both of them.

"Amazing," she breathed. The word fit most of the events of the past week. "You were amazing, too, when we had to deal with your father."

The old man had boiled over with pure hate the first time she'd met him. Ty had gone into the council house alone the morning of his father's return, but she had quickly followed him in. They'd promised each other to fight their battles together, after all.

Though the council house was dark and her eyes slow to adjust from the bright sunlight, there was no mistaking Ty's look—a mixture of frustration and gratitude that sent two messages at the same time: *Jesus, I told you to stay outside* and *Thank God you're here.*

She would have grinned if not for the three centuries of alpha sitting over there like Mount Vesuvius on a very ugly August day.

"You. Dixon," Ty's father snarled.

She pulled her chin up and stood stiff. "Lana."

Old Tyrone's eyes bored into her, and she dipped her eyes in the required sign of submission. It was his pack, after all. She'd give him that. That and nothing else, even if it killed her. But the words he uttered next surprised her.

"You look just like your mother." His voice had a hint of surprise in it, maybe even wonder.

With the nose of my father. That part, she decided to keep to herself.

She couldn't help but lean away from his piercing stare and winced when the floorboard creaked underfoot, betraying her anxiety. The minute she glanced at Ty, though, she felt surer, stronger. Because his eyes held the truth. This wasn't about the past. It was about the future. Their future together.

Ty stood down his father. "This is Lana. My mate." He bit down on the final T like a dog on a juicy bone. "She stays."

The old man didn't answer. He just growled, setting off what seemed to be a telepathic duel in which their eyes did the swordplay, slashing and leaping and parrying in deadly thrusts.

"She's the enemy!" The old man's voice joined in the fight, shaking with anger.

"She's mine!" Ty retorted, immovable as the hills.

As surprised as Lana was at Ty's words, she was more surprised at her reaction. She liked his possessiveness—loved it, in fact. Because he was hers as much as she was his.

"Don't make me do this, Dad," Ty warned.

His father grunted so low that Lana's knees shook. "Do what?"

Ty's lips stayed still, but his eyes blazed with the answer. *Leave. Or fight you. Your choice.*

She held her breath. Ty would do that for her? Leave the ranch? Deep down, she knew he could never start anywhere else. His world was this ranch. But he meant it. She could see it in his stony expression. God, what was she asking of her mate?

She half expected the earth to start shaking, given the sheer power swirling through the room. But it ended in a stalemate with Ty stomping out of the building, Lana firmly in tow.

"There's no dealing with him when he's like that," Ty muttered.

She blew out a long breath, wondering if the old man was ever any other way. The man was a hazardous chemical, a boiling cauldron. Yet Ty had stood up to him.

"You're the one who really stood up to him." Ty said, pulling her attention back to the present. To bed, to the peace of the house, the peace of another night together.

She rubbed her cheek against Ty's chest. *Heaven is here,* she decided. *Right here.*

Ty's deep voice went on, insistent. "No one's ever stood up to him like you did."

"It was you standing up to him," Lana said, running her chin along the stubble of his jaw.

"It was both of us. And if it wasn't for your idea about the land trade, who knows what he would have done."

She allowed herself a small smile. Ty's father had returned to find he'd missed three crises. The rogues were one. Lana, the forbidden Dixon was another. The third was the land dispute: turning a portion of Seymour Ranch over to the state as parkland was a sure recipe for trouble. Lana had mused over the problem for days. How to protect the pack from the outside world?

The answer came to her after Ty drove her to the proposed parkland at Spring Hollow one day, trying to gain a little distance from his father's wrath. The man had been threatening Lana with everything from death to dismemberment and banishment, and the confrontations were getting so bitter, she feared how it would all end.

So she and Ty had taken a time out to visit that lovely piece of land, where a tiny stream watered a wooded grove. The minute they stepped out of the car, she felt the magic of the place. An oasis in the desert, with leafy shade, a babbling brook, and soft earth underfoot. No wonder the late Mrs. Seymour wanted to protect that land. Seduced by the melody of birdsong and rippling water, she and Ty made love under the cottonwoods.

"You don't hear that much any more," he commented as they lay clasped together afterwards.

"Hear what?"

"The spotted owl." He signaled with his eyes the next time it cooed.

It took her twenty minutes to find the bird in the dappled shadows and half a day to realize the implications. A little research quickly paid off. The spotted owl was a threatened species.

"I got it!" Breathless with her discovery, she'd burst in on Ty, his father, and the pack elders in what seemed to be their tenth crisis meeting in three days.

The old alpha met her with his usual scowl. The one that hadn't quite killed her—yet. "If you so much as—"

She cut him off, and even Ty's jaw hung open at that. "I have your solution. Listen."

The room went deathly quiet.

She dug in her heels. "The Seymour Ranch issue. I know what to do."

An elder scoffed audibly, and even Ty gave her an incredulous look.

She spoke directly to him, telling herself it was only Ty she had to face, and not an entire troop of hostile shifters. "The owl, remember?"

Ty gave her a slow nod, his eyes warm with the memory.

"The Mexican spotted owl," she explained for the benefit of the others, "is an endangered species. A protected species."

Nothing but blank and angry faces. They just weren't getting it. Lana all but stomped her foot in exasperation. "We can—I mean, Twin Moon Ranch can declare an adjoining section of its own property a preserve to protect the owls, doubling the size of the Seymour donation. Yes, I mean it," she insisted to the dismissive faces. "But Twin Moon Ranch would retain the right to that land. That will do it!"

Ty seemed to be the only one who was taking her seriously. "Do what?"

"First of all, it demonstrates good will," Lana said, ignoring the old alpha's scowl. Like he'd ever appreciate the subtleties of land negotiations. "If we—*you*—declare the land a nature reserve and vow to keep it off-limits to the public, Seymour Ranch will be forced to do the same."

There, she thought, watching realization dawn over her audience. She savored the moment for all of three seconds before steaming along while she still had momentum. "At the same time, Twin Moon could cede public right of way to that isolated patch of land you own over near Slide Rock State Park."

The gathered men grew darker still. Convincing conservative old wolves to give away land? No easy task, but Lana knew exactly how to handle them. She'd been through the wringer with the elders in her home pack on more than one occasion.

She put her hands up before they could protest. "It's a small parcel with no practical use to the ranch—but it's got scenic value. That's our ace. The public will still gain access to new land, and Mrs. Seymour's wish to set aside Spring Hollow will be respected. Most importantly," she gathered her nerves and looked old Tyrone right in the eye, "the pack will avoid unwanted visitors. It's a win-win for everyone."

She folded her arms and shut her mouth. There. Let them chew on that.

There was a collective scratching of heads, a few surprised stares, but no rebuttals, no complaints. Just a weighty silence that stretched on and on.

"And you think they'll go for this?" one of the elders ventured.

"I know they'll go for this," Lana said. "I can draw up a formal proposal and have it ready for the state authorities by tomorrow." *Plus copies for Seymour Ranch and the usual environmental watchdogs*, she made a mental note to herself, already working out the details. She'd need the original deeds, and maps, and a thousand other things, but that part was all routine. "They'll take the deal, believe me."

Nobody seemed too inclined to believe her, but then again, no one was protesting her plan. Not even the mighty old alpha.

"How'd you figure this all out?" Ty had asked, once he'd found the hinge to his jaw.

"It's what I did at home, silly. It's my job."

The elders frowned. Did she really dare speak to the upcoming alpha that way? But Ty just cracked into a grin that was all love layered with pride, and for the next minute, all Lana did was drink it in. Forget the elders, forget his father.

Mate. My mate. She still couldn't fathom her luck.

Ty's father tilted his head as if seeing her in a new light. "That will do," he grunted, dismissing her.

She managed a firm nod, then made for the door. She got as far as the second hitching post on the right before leaning into it, hard. Jesus. Had she really stood up to the old alpha?

Her pulse was still racing when the council house door opened and Cody came out. His eyes sparkled as he came up to her, like he'd just surfed down the biggest, baddest wave of his life.

"I'd kiss you if my brother wouldn't skin me alive," he said, coming right up to her. "Oh, what the heck," he said, glancing left and right. Then he leaned in and gave her a peck on the cheek. "You did it!" He was like Huck Finn in a second skin, always excited to embark on a fabulous adventure that was sure to go wrong a hundred different times. She wondered if he'd ever grow up.

If only he was aware of the obstacles still ahead of them. Lana didn't know what the hurdles would be, exactly, but they were out there. The only constant in the tumultuous world of a wolf pack was trouble. Sooner or later, it'd be back, for sure.

Ty came out then, and all her worries fled. With her mate, she could accomplish anything. *They* could accomplish anything.

The door slammed against the wall as Ty's father stormed out of the council house like the back edge of a hurricane: all dark and mumbly, yet weary. He pulled up two steps away from Lana, and though he fixed her with those laser eyes—just like Ty's, yet nothing at all like Ty's—the hand he raised was pointing right. Lana followed it to another low-slung building with dusty panes of glass.

"That one," he barked. "That office. I want her where I can keep an eye on her," he snapped, then stormed away.

Cody gave Lana another winning grin, then ambled off, leaving her and Ty alone. She caught her mate in a loose hug and leaned her forehead against his chest. God, it felt good to be so close. To know she'd never have to let go again.

"Throwing down a challenge, is he?" she managed, picturing the musty files the old alpha would be heaping on her desk soon enough.

Ty shook his head and pulled her flush against his body, ignoring the elders filing past. "He's already sold on you, sweetheart. Not that he'll admit it." Then he released her and turned firmly in the direction of his house.

Our house, he insisted, pulling her closer.

She slipped a hand into his back pocket as they walked side by side. Home. The sweetest four letter word ever. She could stay—not just as Ty's mate, but in her own right.

"But no more work 'til you're fully healed," he added.

This time, she didn't mind the bossy tone one bit. "I am healed," she insisted. "Or just about."

"Well, no work until we've had some time for us."

"That, my love, will never be enough."

But hell, they'd certainly given it their best shot over the past days. In the cabin, up at his lookout, in every room of the house. And now they rolled slowly out of bed, still tingling from their lovemaking. They shifted and loped into the night, Ty's long stride perfectly matching her quick footfalls. She was glad to work her stiff limbs and even gladder to be running side by side with her mate. The hushed voices coming from the desert on this moonlit night were no lies. Ty was her destined mate, all hers. Now and forever.

They nestled together on Ty's hill and lifted their muzzles as one. To warm up, they let out a mournful howl that acknowledged the pain of the past, then moved on to a long, happy howl for the future, one that sang on and on into the night. Around them, the desert listened, maybe even shed a sentimental tear. Destiny was smiling on them, and she never wanted it to end.

Her lips curled in a canine grin as she squeezed closer to his side. There didn't have to be an end.

This was only the beginning.

Other books by Anna Lowe

The Wolves of Twin Moon Ranch

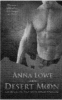

Desert Hunt (the Prequel)

Desert Moon (Book 1)

Desert Wolf 1 (a short story)

Desert Wolf 2 (a short story)

Desert Wolf 3 (a short story)

Desert Blood (Book 2)

Desert Fate (Book 3)

Desert Heart (Book 4)

Happily Mated After (a short story)

Desert Yule (a short story)

Desert Rose (Book 5)

Desert Roots (Book 6)

Serendipity Adventure Romance

Off the Charts

Uncharted

Entangled

Windswept

Adrift

Travel Romance

Veiled Fantasies

Island Fantasies

visit www.annalowebooks.com

Sneak Peek I: Desert Blood

Heather Luth knows nothing about the paranormal world until one awful night changes everything. Now she's on the run—straight into the arms of forbidden love. Her mind knows better than to fall for Cody Hawthorne's sunny smile and mesmerizing voice, but her heart—and destiny—have other ideas.

On the surface, Cody is warm, witty, and fun, but beneath his carefree facade, Heather sees a real man struggling to break free. Day by day, Heather and Cody grow closer and closer, unable to resist their simmering passion—while day by day, a serial murderer closes in on his prey. Duty fights desire; fear wrestles trust as the human world clashes with the paranormal in a tale of forbidden love.

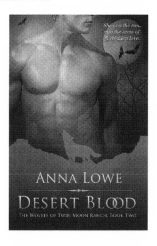

Sneak Peek: Chapter One

Fleeing wasn't the hard part; knowing when to stop was. But how far was far enough? How fast?

Heather didn't know. All she cared about was getting away. Red-eyed and bleary, stretched beyond exhaustion, she drove until the thick woods and hills of the East gave way to the infinite landscape of the West, with no plan but to get away from the beast who lusted after her blood.

She nearly rushed through this barren landscape entirely, a mere blip on a map she had long since given up on following. But from one mile to the next, the frantic urge to run was replaced by a warm, safe sensation, as if she'd flipped a shower tap from icy cold to blissfully hot. She let her dusty orange VW roll to a stop on the side of the road then got out and turned in a slow circle, scanning the scene. What was it about this place?

The sun rose boldly over the high altitude desert, highlighting a razorback horizon wrinkled by time. A pale crescent moon hung low over the hills, dripping pale pink light on the brush below. All of it was perfumed by sage and pine, beargrass and buttercup. The grandeur of the scene spoke of time—eons of it, whispering on a breath of wind.

This. This was the place. Even with her eyes closed, she could feel the rightness of it. This place would become her home.

A falcon wheeled overhead, and its sharp cry split the air. Heather blinked, snapping herself back to reality. Wait—there was no home. There was only escape. But for now, this would have to do. No use in running blindly any more. She needed to make a plan, to think things through.

She forced in a deep breath and tried to take stock. Cash was getting low, and she was afraid to use a card because that could be traced, right? And the man who'd attacked her—the monster who'd attacked her—was capable of anything.

She ran her hands over her arms, trying to still a shiver. She needed a plan. Soon.

No, she needed a plan right now. But what?

Work. A safe place. Those were the priorities. She needed to find work and lay low in a place as far off the beaten track as she could find.

A place like this.

She scanned the open, unfenced scrubland that no one seemed to claim as their own. What kind of teaching job would she ever find in the desert? Teaching was all she'd ever done, all she ever wanted to do.

But this wasn't about wanting. This was about survival. She could wait tables, clean floors, whatever it took.

She took one more look around and nodded, making up her mind. If nothing else, this place was fitting. It was open, endless, and brutally honest. Death might be hovering out on the fringes, but at least it couldn't sneak up on her here.

In her first decisive action since fleeing Pittsburgh, she slid back into the car, reached past the empty coffee cups on the passenger side floor, and dug out the map she hadn't checked since Texas. Where was she, exactly? Somewhere in Arizona— that much she knew. But where?

She glanced up at the scenery, down at the map, and up again. There'd been a town a couple of miles back, and that was as good a place to start as any. She gunned the engine to life and turned the car around. Twenty miles later, she was there: a tiny no-name town on the fringes of a slightly bigger, no-name town.

Heather checked into a motel that was only marginally less dusty than her car, slept thirty-six hours straight, then pulled herself together, one frayed thread at a time. A friendly wait-ress at a diner got her started with a phone book and a few names. It took dozens of calls, but within a couple of days, she found a tiny bungalow to rent on the edge of town and a job—a teaching job, even. A one-room schoolhouse on a lonely outpost of a ranch had a last-minute opening. In the interview, Heather rattled off her qualifications then rushed through the reason she'd left her job in Pennsylvania so abruptly.

"A stalker," she said. That was as close to the truth as she dared utter aloud.

It was enough—she got the job.

"It's only for two months," said Lana, the woman from the ranch. "Until our regular teacher comes back from emergency family leave."

"Two months is perfect." She'd catch her breath, earn a little cash, and then move on. Because sooner or later, the beast who hunted her would come looking. That much she knew.

Sneak Peek: Chapter Two

The schoolhouse was a slanted old adobe, full of charm, if a little run-down, and the job was a bucking bronco, determined to pitch her off. But Heather was just as determined to hang on to this one scrap of sanity within her reach, even if it was the teaching challenge of her life. Eleven students, spread through all grades—from emerging readers to rowdy fifth graders. It took two bouncy weeks for her to convince that bronc to finally let her take the reins, but she did it. She found reserves of patience she didn't know she had, spent hours prepping lessons, and fell into bed exhausted each night. But she did it.

Once the kids settled into a new routine, everything got easier. Mornings were quieter, afternoons smoother. Right now, the kids were at their learning stations in pairs, working quietly while Heather went over essay writing with two third-graders.

A shriek drew her attention to the back of the schoolhouse, and she looked up then ducked on instinct. Something swept straight over her head, brushing her hair. Becky was screaming; Timmy was pointing. The room erupted into noise as the other kids joined in with high-pitched squeals that resounded off the walls.

"A bat! A bat!"

It made another pass, and Heather swiped the air over her head.

"Miss Luth! Miss Luth! A bat!"

She followed the silky black form until it perched on a high shelf. A tiny, pink tongue darted out and lapped at the air between them. She could swear its beady eyes were studying her. Something about the bat seemed...evil. She held back a shudder and forced herself into action. "Timmy, get me a towel!"

For once, Timmy did as he was told. Heather approached the bat, towel in hand, kids cheering her on.

"Get it, Miss Luth! Get it!"

"Be careful, Miss Luth!"

Telling herself it was only a bat—one little bat—she lunged, but the bat was a step ahead, weaving and diving around the classroom. The noise level surged to a new peak, like a boxing arena at the first sight of blood.

"Everything okay?" A voice came from the doorway, completely unperturbed. It was soothing, like the sound of waves over a smooth, sandy shore. The voice warmed her from the inside even before she spun and spotted the newcomer.

"Cody! Cody!" the children cried.

Heather's stomach did a flip. It was him. The one she'd noticed around the ranch. The one she couldn't *not* notice.

The ranch seemed to be a breeding ground for gorgeous men, but this one was in a class of his own. Lean, blond, relaxed. Most of the others came in the strong-but-silent, earthy category, but this one should be bobbing on a surfboard, wiping salt water out of his eyes. He seemed in no hurry whatsoever, as if today was just another great day of many.

The kids whipped themselves into a new frenzy, pointing at the bat, high on another shelf.

"Cody! A bat! A bat!" Timmy jumped up and down on his desk, and a panicked Becky threw herself into the man's arms. He scooped her up and patted her back while Timmy shouted. "I saw it first! I saw it first!"

"Timmy, sit down!" Heather shot him her best teacher look.

Cody whispered to Becky, bringing a smile back to her face. Then he pointed at Timmy, eyes sparkling with mischief. "Do I know you?"

That voice could soothe a thousand wailing babies. She wanted to wrap it around her like a blanket.

"Cody! It's me, Timmy!"

He looked at the boy then right into Heather's eyes. Her heart skipped a beat. "I swear I don't know this child."

"Cody!" Timmy protested.

The man tousled Timmy's hair and lowered Becky back to her seat. Then he stepped up to Heather, eyes utterly, unfailingly devoted to hers. She caught a breath and held it. He'd never been this close before. Never done anything but wave a friendly hello from across the way. She'd had to force herself away every time because the urge to stop and talk— to look, to get closer, maybe even to touch—was damn near impossible to resist.

Now he was inches away. Big, broad—but not too much of either. Just right. The nick in one ear was the only part of him that wasn't perfect. She caught his scent, and it was an ocean breeze gone walkabout in the desert.

She gave herself an inner slap. No, no, no! Men were not to be trusted. Not ever again.

Not even this one? a small voice in her cried.

Especially not this one! came the slamming reply.

"Cody, get the bat!" the kids urged. "Get it! Get it!" Pandemonium once again.

A second voice boomed into the doorway, deep and gravelly. "What the hell is going on here?"

Without thinking, Heather wheeled, slammed her hands onto her hips, and shot out a reply. "Watch your language! This is a school!" For a moment, she felt like her old self—in command, not only of the students but herself. The Heather from before the nightmare.

When the second man stepped in, the air pressure in the room immediately rose, as if a storm system were squeezing itself through the doorway. Scampering feet pounded the wooden floorboards as kids rushed back to their seats and stood stiffly at attention. She could swear everyone was holding their breath—including the bat.

The man's piercing eyes glowed with anger. The old Heather might have stood her ground, but the Heather she'd become wavered and took a step back. She might have melted onto the floor, mortified, if Cody hadn't stepped between them, practically growling.

Her shoulders slumped. Oh God, the second man was the ranch boss. She'd lose her job. She'd be thrown out. She'd—

"Don't mind my brother," Cody said softly.

That tenor was magic, sending a warm, secure rush her way. Heather straightened slightly and looked from Cody to the other one. Ty, that was his name. Were they really brothers? One was a thundercloud; the other, pure sunshine. As opposite as opposites can be.

Before she knew it, Ty whisked the towel out of her hands and stepped toward the bat. He must have fixed it with that laser of a gaze because the bat submitted without so much as lifting a wing. When Ty scooped it up and stepped outside, moving quickly down the flagstone path, the whole room exhaled.

Heather leaned against the wall, suddenly drained. "Five minute break, kids." They broke into gleeful cries and ran out to the playground, leaving Heather and Cody alone.

"My brother does have a soft spot, you know." Cody grinned. "It comes out every second year or so."

Definitely opposites, those two. She'd take this one in an instant and worship him like the sun.

His eyes were studying the blackboard, reading the words. "My dream home?" He grinned like Huck Finn, but all grown up. Very grown up.

She would bet anything he'd been like Timmy as a kid. Sweet, energetic, mischievous. And now, sweet, studly, and mischievous. She'd give anything to make like Becky and hide herself against that chest.

Heather cleared her throat. "Geometry. They have to find shapes in the house, and then draw their own dream homes."

"And this one is yours?" He nodded to the board.

The U-shaped ranch she'd been kidding herself about for years? She shrugged the notion away. "Nah. Just an example."

He chuckled. "Right."

God, that smile could make her forget everything. Like the fact that she'd sworn off men. Like the fact that she had eleven rambunctious kids to supervise instead of standing there, letting goose bumps tickle her skin.

Like the fact that the last man she'd let this close nearly killed her.

But with those gold-brown eyes caressing hers, she just might forget.

"Cody!" Ty growled from outside, breaking whatever spell had wafted in with the wind.

"Gotta go," Cody sighed. He stood looking at her for a long, mournful minute—a kid watching the ice cream truck pull away before he got a scoop. "Gotta go," he repeated, eyes sliding shut. Seemed to Heather he'd aimed that whisper at himself.

And then he was gone, leaving the room emptier than it had ever felt before.

More from Anna Lowe

Check out the other side of Anna Lowe with a series even die-hard paranormal fans rave about: the Serendipity Adventure Romance series. You can try it FREE with *Off The Charts*, a short story prequel you can receive for FREE by signing up for Anna Lowe's newsletter at *annalowebooks.com*!

Listen to what a few Twin Moon fans have to say about this new series:

- *This is as HOT as her shifter series. For those who want spicy without paranormal, this is a perfect start. I can't wait to read more about these characters.*

- *I'm enjoying Anna's new series just as much as I do her Wolves of Twin Moon Ranch series.*

- *It's not my normal genre but I do love Anna Lowe's romance books because of the great way she writes. I am really happy this book was the same great style.*

- *Uncharted is different from Anna's Wolves of Twin Moon Ranch but I enjoyed the story just as well.*

About the Author

USA Today and Amazon bestselling author Anna Lowe loves putting the "hero" back into heroine and letting location ignite a passionate romance. She likes a heroine who is independent, intelligent, and imperfect – a woman who is doing just fine on her own. But give the heroine a good man – not to mention a chance to overcome her own inhibitions – and she'll never turn down the chance for adventure, nor shy away from danger.

Anna is a middle school teacher who loves dogs, sports, and travel – and letting those inspire her fiction. Once upon a time, she was a long-distance triathlete and soccer player. Nowadays, she finds her balance with yoga, writing, and family time with her husband and young children.

On any given weekend, you might find her hiking in the mountains or hunched over her laptop, working on her latest story. Either way, the day will end with a chunk of dark chocolate and a good read.

Visit AnnaLoweBooks.com